# FRANKIE'S UNLAWFUL CARNAL KNOWLEDGE

## A NOVEL BY

## L. KURT EDDY

An Idea Machine Output Publication

Published in 2018 by Idea Machine Output LLC

Idea Machine Output books may be purchased for educational, business, or sale promotional use. For information, please email info@ideamachineoutput.com

Also, don't be a Frankie.

ISBN-13: 978-1-947831-00-1
ISBN-10: 1947831003
LICCN: 2017953306

To Floyd.
You read this and you liked it.
You sick fuck.

*A man without wits is like a man without balls;*
*He might as well find himself being nothing at all.*

- Doctor Circus

# THE 1<sup>ST</sup> ACT OF THE GREATEST PORNO EVER MADE

His name was Frankie Wood. That wasn't the name on his birth certificate, though. To his mother and father and the federal government, he was known as Francis Collinwood, but he didn't like that name anymore.

He'd picked Frankie Wood because he believed it fit the persona he now exuded better. It was the perfect name for a sleazeball, which, when he began, was something he was pretending to be. Now, he'd been pretending for so long, a sleazeball is what he'd become.

That is why to everyone he worked with he was Frankie Wood, Director, Writer, and Producer. It was a fitting name for what he was doing and what he wanted to do. He was a pornographer, plain and simple, and all he wanted was to make the greatest porno ever made.

At least he used to. Now, he honestly didn't know what he wanted.

His career had become a jumbled mess. He hated everything about what he was doing. He hated the talent he worked with, from the actors to the behind-the-scenes guys. He hated the ideas he was given. He even hated himself.

Really how could he not hate himself? All the hatred he had for what he was doing had to trickle down to somewhere and he was right there on the bottom of it all. He was at the base of the funnel that accumulated the piss and shit and cum and it was beginning to show. It might as well have been smeared all over his face.

He, at some point he couldn't place, had decided that maybe he should stop caring about what he looked like. He had let his once bleach blonde hair grow out. His dark roots were showing through. He also hadn't shaved. This was barely noticeably, though, since he couldn't really grow anything other than a mustache.

It wasn't a normal mustache, mind you, it was a skeevy mustache, as thin as it was long. It was also, to make matters worse, unkempt. The hairs of it seemed to fray outward as though it was cut from something thicker than it was. It wasn't though. It just grew that way. It sat above his lip like some sort of perverted caterpillar amidst a sea of stubble. He knew it looked ridiculous, but he was too putout to care.

He'd stopped giving a fuck awhile ago. That was around the time he started wearing Hawaiian shirts all the time. He found they were the cheapest items to buy at thrift stores and so he just bought a shit-ton. He needed to wear something, so why not that? Beggars can't be choosers. Or something like that.

The truly unfortunate thing about all of this was that

his faux self-deprecation was starting to seep into his work. Not only had he stopped caring about how he looked, but he stopped caring about how his films looked too. It was a slippery slope to fall down, but falling down he was. He could barely even be bothered to show up to direct the piece-of-shit films he was directing, and the damn things were being shot in his garage, downstairs.

That's where he found himself at that particular moment in time: he was laying on his back thinking about how he didn't want to be bothered with directing whatever piece-of-shit he was supposed to helm.

The sun had come up and he could hear the commotion coming from downstairs. He found it strange how it took him so long to realize it was a shoot day. He'd been directing for years, yet still it took him a moment to comprehend that the noises he was hearing from downstairs were probably craft services setting up.

He found himself hoping, against hope, that no one would come up to bug him about it. He wished that they would just shoot the fucking thing and then he could watch what they'd done later and shit all over it, but still inevitably release it. He'd always release it. It didn't matter how much it sucked. People would buy it as long as it got them off.

His wishes weren't met though and soon he heard someone make their way up the creaking stairs and knock on the door.

"Yeah?" Frankie asked as he realized he'd missed the bed by a few feet and was lying on the floor. He was still dressed in the same Hawaiian shirt he was wearing the previous day.

"Hey, boss, it's time for us to start," a voice from behind the door said. "They're asking for you."

"Is that you, Miles?" Frankie asked. He knew it wasn't as soon as he asked him. It had taken him a moment to realize that the voice from the other end of the door had a heavy Spanish accent and that Miles didn't have one.

"No sir," the voice said, in that accent of his, "I was just asked to get you."

"Alright, alright, yeah," said Frankie, trying to sound as dismissive as possible. "I'll be down in a minute."

The voice on the other end didn't say anything, but Frankie could hear footsteps walking away.

Once he was sure the footsteps had receded he got up and went to his bathroom. It was a wreck in there. Flashes of what had happened the night prior slipped into his mind as he looked around the bathroom. Coke had been done here. Lots of it. Maybe some H too, it was hard to tell.

He put a glob of toothpaste onto his fingers and rubbed it in his mouth, against his teeth. The mere taste of the spearmint or peppermint or whatever-the-fuck-mint made him want to wretch. He didn't though. That was a matter of pride for him. No matter how fucked up he got, he would never puke the next day. It was the one part of the old code he once kept that he still adhered too.

Once he was done with the bullshit ritual of making

4

his breath smell pleasant, he debated changing shirts. Changing shirts would mean that he would have to do laundry. He decided to keep the one he was wearing on. No one would notice anyway.

He then made his way downstairs and saw that calamity was already ensuing. The place was full of people, some of whom he didn't even know. There were the bullshit craft service people and some of the crew, but there were also *other people*. These were the people that Frankie called "the hangers-on." They were the types of people that just wanted to see some dicks and some cunts and some tits and said dicks going into said cunts and cumming on said tits afterwards. Maybe they'd see someone bust off on a pretty lady's face. Who knew? No one. That's why they were there, to see what (or who) would go down.

Frankie abhorred such people. If he'd been in a better mindset (i.e.: not hungover off booze and coke and who knows what) then he would have kicked their asses out. Instead he did nothing.

That seemed to bother everybody. A strange hush went over the crowd when Frankie came down, as though they expected him to speak, but when he didn't say a word, they kept holding their breaths.

As Frankie went out to the garage he was worried they might hold their breaths until they died. He knew he wouldn't be so lucky, though.

Once he was in the garage he walked over to his little director's chair and sat down. It was placed behind the fancy-dancy camera they had just bought and he could see what they were planning on capturing as well as what would be in the shot. He sized it up to make sure it looked good and deemed it "good enough." It wasn't great, but he didn't feel like complaining today.

"Are we rolling?" Frankie asked as he lit up a smoke.

"Yes, for the billionth time," Miles, his best friend in the whole wide world, said sarcastically, as though that was the punch line to some joke Frankie didn't understand.

"Fuck you," Frankie said to Miles as though he'd said it a thousand times. He then sat up in his chair, motioned to everyone else and then shouted "Action!" as loudly as he could muster.

He then leaned back, uneasy about what was about to unfold, and closed his eyes.

In the darkness of his mind he could hear a door knocking.

"Who is it?" Rachel asked. It wasn't really Rachel, though. It was some character she'd concocted. The character sounded ditsy and way too southern.

"I've got a delivery here for a… Miss Popper," he could hear James say. Again, though, that wasn't the James he knew, but a character. It was a character that seemed like he was going out of his way to sound black.

Frankie could then hear stiletto shoes clip-clop to an unseen door that opens with a slight creaking sound. Frankie wished he would have tried the stage door before they used it. He also wished he would have okayed the shoes Rachel had chosen to wear; she could never walk properly in heels that were too high.

"I'm Miss Popper," Rachel said, apparently as Miss Popper.

"Cherry Popper," James said, as though he were waiting for a laugh. None came. And none would. Viewers would probably skip past this part anyway, so really, it didn't matter.

"Yep, that's me," Rachel said, dropping the accent for a second, before picking it back up, "And who might you be?"

"My name is Ash Ripper," James said.

Frankie flinched when he heard that and rolled his eyes behind his lids. He was kicking himself for not proofreading the script before hand, but how on earth could he have known it would be that bad?

"Oh," Rachel said with all the faux-excitement she could muster. "And what is it you want from me?"

"Well a lot of things, ma'am," James said. Frankie swore he heard James wink, but that would be impossible. "But the reason I'm here," James continued, sloppily. "Is 'cuz I've got a couch for you."

"Ooooh," Rachel said, half-confused, half-sexy. "Is it my new couch?"

Frankie could hear Rachel flubbing a line from a mile away. She did it mere feet from him and so it hit his ears like a ton of bricks.

"Yes?" James said, clearly thrown off by the fucked-up line. "Ma'am," he then added, as though that would correct the damage that had been done.

"Good," Rachel said, picking up where she let the scene leave off. "Well bring it in. Please."

Frankie just listened on, hoping that the scene would suddenly get good. All he heard was the sound of James struggling with a couch as he tries to make it fit through the flimsy stage door. It became too much for Frankie to bear.

He opened his eyes. The tableau that he was privy too was all that he imagined: a complete and utter shit-show.

"Cut!" Frankie shouted. "Dear fucking god," he muttered to himself, loudly enough for everyone to hear.

Before anyone could cut the tape or stop acting, Frankie was on the set looking around. He eyed everything and realized that absolutely nothing had been planned properly.

"Miles!" He called out to the crew.

Miles Johnson, Frankie's best friend and a co-producer on all of his productions, walks up to Frankie. Frankie was immediately taken aback by how clean Miles looked. It was almost egregious.

Not only was Miles clean-cut, but he also seemed more put together as a whole. When he walked up to Frankie he was ready to work. He had a clipboard in his hand (with the script within it) and a stopwatch around his neck, as though he was keeping time of something. The way he rushed up to Frankie was enough to make Frankie feel like shit for not caring about the production in the slightest.

"It's about a minute and a half, two minutes, maybe," Miles said as he approached.

8

"No, no," Frankie said, half-remembering the rule he made about keeping most exposition to under two minutes. "It's this fucking set man."

"What about it?" Miles went to his clipboard as though he was going to write a note down.

"It's just not made for this scene," Frankie said with a sigh. "I mean who the fuck thought we could fit a couch through this door?" Frankie kicked the stage door for emphasis.

"Well I don't know, we thought it would work," Miles said. "We did ask you about it, remember?"

"Who the fuck wrote this shit, Miles?" Frankie asked, choosing to ignore Miles' question that implied that this might be his fault.

"What do you mean, chief?" Miles asked, genuinely perplexed.

"Who the fuck wrote *this* shit," Frankie repeated, waving his hands around so that his point might be made.

"Um," Miles said, feigning like he needed to actually think about it, like it wasn't just there on his clipboard, "I think James did."

"James?" Frankie asked in disbelief. "James?" He repeated as though he'd misheard (he hadn't). He then pointed to James. "You mean *that* James?"

"Yes," Miles said, as though he had done something wrong.

"What the fuck?" Frankie asked to no one in particular. "Did I okay that?" He asked Miles directly.

"Yeah," Miles said with confidence. "Him and

Rachel came to you with the idea and James wrote the script."

Frankie looked at Miles as though what Miles had said was brand new information.

"You read it yesterday, man," Miles said.

"God damn it," Frankie said. To anyone who heard it, it sounded as though he was pissed off at Miles or maybe James. Really, though, he was just pissed off at himself. He couldn't believe he let the slithery shit of a script slip through.

Frankie then looked around at everything that was happening before him. He looked to the crew and then the cameras. He saw the set, the couch, and the fucking door. Then his eyes came to rest on the cast. His eyes stopped on them like some sort of divining rod. As he looked upon them a crazy notion struck him.

He grabbed Miles by the shoulder and moved him off to the side, away from the earshot of the rest of the cast and crew.

"Hey," Frankie whispered to Miles once they were far enough away from all the hubbub. "Do you know if James and Rachel are fucking on the side?"

"I don't know," Miles said, in a whisper. It was clear that this line of questioning would make him uncomfortable if Frankie were to continue down it.

"Well find out, will you?" Frankie asked, before he hunkered down as though to shade them from any prying eyes (this was done more for Miles' benefit than Frankie's). "*Discreetly.*" He then winked and clicked his tongue for some reason.

As they were having this semi-private moment (all eyes were on them, after all) a crew member approached them. Frankie was sure he'd seen the man before, but he couldn't be sure.

"We're ready to go whenever you are, Mr. Wood," the crew member told Frankie. It was then Frankie realized that this crewmember was responsible for the voice that had beckoned him downstairs earlier.

"Yeah?" Frankie asked, opting to ignore the rudeness that the crew member had clearly shown. "You guys got the couch in and everything?"

"Yes sir," the crew member said, somewhat nervously.

"Alright," Frankie said as he put a cigarette into his mouth and lit it. "Go ahead and roll it then."

"Roll it!" said the crew member as he walked off.

"Rolling!" shouted another crew member. As he heard that, Frankie realized that maybe the crew member he had been speaking to previously was not, in fact, the one who woke him up earlier. It could have been the guy who shouted "Rolling."

"Hey!" Frankie then yelled to the original crew member.

"Yes sir?" the crewmember replied as he turned back to face Frankie.

"I fucking say when to roll it, alright?" Frankie tried to sound stern, but he knew he just looked like some asshole trying to prove a point.

"Yes sir," said the crew member, obviously feeling the same way about Frankie that Frankie felt about himself. Frankie took note of his subordinate's tone, but opted to not do anything about it, at least not then.

"Good," said Frankie. "Fucking roll it then. Let's get into places, yeah?"

He then motioned for James and Rachel to do whatever it was they thought they were doing. Once they appeared to be where they were supposed to be, Frankie went back to where his chair was, sat down, and closed his eyes.

"Action!" he shouted.

After a moment he could hear springs on the couch begin to bounce with an annoying squeak.

"Oh," Rachel said, getting back into her ditsy, southern character. "This couch has some bounce to it."

"That's cool," James said, giving more gravitas to his character than the script he was performing deserved. "Could I get you to sign this?"

Frankie heard a piece of paper being loudly unfolded. He could tell that James dropped the pen.

"Sure, I could," overly-southern Rachel said. "First, why don't you come and try this couch out with me?"

Frankie couldn't help but rub the bridge of his nose, up to his eye sockets, with his thumb and his forefinger. As far as he was concerned the shit he was hearing was utter hack (and that was putting it lightly).

"Sure," James said.

Frankie could hear couch springs compress.

"This couch sure is comfy," James said, almost making it sound believable. The way the springs

L. KURT EDDY

sounded, though, made Frankie know that James was full of shit.

"I know," Rachel said. "But it must've sure been heavy. I saw you struggling with it when you were bringing it up from your mover's truck and you sure are strong."

That line struck Frankie like a sour note. He opened his eyes and when he did, he saw Miles standing there. Miles thrust a script into his hands, as though he could read Frankie's mind and knew that's what he needed.

Frankie took the script and feverishly flipped through it, trying to find the location of the awful scene they were currently doing.

"Yeah, it was very heavy," James said as Frankie caught up to what he was saying.

"Do you mind if I feel your *big* muscles, Mr. Ripper?" Rachel asked.

Frankie rolled his eyes as he read what she said as she said it. He couldn't believe they were actually working off of the shitty script he had in his hands. He scoffed audibly before he threw the script on the floor and closed his eyes again. He didn't want to read further, he knew it would just drive him further into disappointment.

"No, I don't mind if you feel my muscles," James said. To his credit, he really was bringing all of his acting chops to the table. It was just unfortunate that the table was serving bitter scraps that weren't worth the pablum they were being served with. "And please," James then said, "call me 'Ash.'"

13

"Okay, *Ash*," Rachel said. She couldn't sound more faux-seductive if she had tried.

Frankie could hear Rachel giggle in the most horrendous way. It was like nails on a chalkboard. It was like batteries through a cheese grater. Frankie could feel a migraine coming on.

"What you laughing 'bout?" James asked. It was as though he dropped the theatre kid in him and decided to go back to the full-black cliché.

"Nothing," Rachel said as she let out that horrendous giggle again. "It's just that my daddy would've killed me if he would've known that when I came to college on his dime that I would invite a big, strong *black* man into my dorm room."

Frankie couldn't help but cringe. He didn't know if it was because he knew where the over-done scene was going or if it was the way Rachel had decided to hit 'black.' His head shook, almost as if it knew before his mind did that he was producing something absolutely wretched.

"Well," James began, "I'm not all black, you know. I feel like you should know that."

Frankie's ears perked up when he heard the possibility of a new spin on things.

"What?" Rachel asked.

"Do you want to see?" James asked back to her.

Frankie, for a second, felt electricity move up through his body. Something brand new might be about to transpire. Perhaps this wasn't the same rinky-dink porno Frankie was used to throwing together.

14

"Yes, please," Rachel said. Her faux-excitement had turned to real excitement.

Frankie could hear James' pants unzip. He could conjure up in his mind the image of James pulling his dick out of the fly and wielding it like the weapon it was.

"You see this spot right there?" James said. "That's my white spot." It was clear to Frankie that James was pointing to the little white birthmark he had on his dick. It was pink and small; a sharp contrast to the rest of his cock.

"Oh, I sure do," Rachel said with a giggle. "Mmmmm, can I touch it?"

"Of course, baby," James said.

That's when all the electricity that Frankie had thought he felt left his body. The amount of disappointment coursing through him at that moment was unfathomable. There wasn't a scale that exists in the world that could weigh the hatred he had for the bullshit he had just heard.

It was made all the worse when he heard Rachel's unbelievably fake moaning and ensued. She really laid it on thick.

"Put it in your mouth, baby," James said to Rachel before there was a sucking sound. If there was one good thing that Frankie could say about her, it was that she could really make sucking a cock sound good. But it sounded too good. It was unbelievable. The way she moaned between sucks and the sighs of elation she hummed out while her mouth was around James' shaft, were just sounds that no one who'd had their cock sucked before had ever heard. She was playing too much to the audience. She wasn't in the scene. It disgusted Frankie.

It took everything in him to keep listening and to not call for a stop to it all. Anger was searing within him. It could surely be seen on his face. Somehow, he managed to hold it in, though.

"Does that feel good?" Rachel asked after she'd come up for air.

"Yeah, baby," James said. "That feels real good." James sounded a little too comfortable for Frankie's taste.

"I can taste how good if feels," Rachel said in her stupid accent.

Frankie squirmed in his chair. What the fuck did that even mean? How the fuck did that make any sense? It was bullshit. All of it was bullshit.

"Yeah, baby," James said. He really said "baby" again. Frankie wished he could switch it up a bit, but he knew that would be asking too much of James. "Put it back in your mouth."

Frankie had to mentally restrain himself then. That line was so hack to him. It had been done a million times before. Sure, it was porn, but was it Frankie Wood Porn? Frankie didn't think so.

Cheesy moaning and sucking sounds could be heard resounding off the set walls. Hell, they were echoing off garage walls. (That's how over-exaggerated they were.)

Frankie decided he needed to open his eyes and see

what exactly the camera was shooting. As per usually, Rachel had no concept of angles. Frankie found himself in a funk.

"Rachel, turn your head," Frankie said in a harsh whisper. He got the side-eye from the sound guy, but waved him off.

Frankie looked back to the screen jutting off the camera and could see that Rachel did not hear him.

"Turn your head," Frankie said, slightly louder. He felt it was quiet enough to not be picked up in audio, but the sound guy, again, looked over to him.

Rachel, though, apparently didn't hear him that time, either. He knew that couldn't be true, however. He knew Rachel must have heard him. The sound guy was giving him guff, for Christ's sake.

"Turn your fucking head, Rachel!" he nearly shouted. He figured that if no one else gave a fuck about it than why should he? He was only pretending to care at that moment and if no one would help him keep up the façade than why should he care?

The yell seemed to work and Rachel turned her head.

"Good," Frankie said as he looked into the little, half-assed monitor. "That looks good."

Frankie then shut his eyes again.

He listened as the fake moaning and sucking continued on and on and on, seemingly without an end.

He tried to imagine what must be happening through his shut eyes. He tried to see it as the actors (clearly) saw it. But it wasn't his first rodeo. He could hear the crew members shift. They would move a bit and then wait a beat and then move a little more. He could hear the crinkling of papers. He could hear the sound of the boom mic moving. It reached a head when he smelled the smell of marijuana waft up from somewhere.

He had a strict no-smoking policy on set. It had to be necessary to smoke. (That really meant that it was a luxury reserved for any actors in the scene or for him and him alone.) If anyone else did, it might fuck up the shot. No one else knew how to handle such things.

He opened his eyes and darted them around. He tried to find the culprit, but the dope-smoker went unfound. Whoever it was had concealed themselves well. His eyes darted hither-and-tither, trying to find the sad soul who had broken the rule, but they found no one. Perhaps he had just imagined it.

Now that his eyes were open though, they moved to the scene that was transpiring. He saw that Rachel had her mouth around James' cock and was working it with much skill. Skill is not enough, though. Skill doesn't sell fucking videos. Her skill was just doing one thing: getting James off. Frankie needed to get the whole world off. What Rachel was doing would simply not do the job.

Frankie leaned up in his chair.

"Alright, that's enough Rach," he said as he positioned himself in a directorial manner. "Just go ahead and move up to his chest."

He then watched as she moved her lips up his shaft,

to his cock's head, and then began to kiss his belly.

"Good," he said when he saw this.

Rachel kissed her way up James' six-pack abs.

"Good," Frankie said, again.

She moved up to the nipples placed perfectly on his muscular chest by a favorable god and began to suck on them.

"Good," Frankie coached, for a third time.

Rachel stayed on his nipples though, she began to moan and pant as though she was sucking his dick.

"Move," Frankie said, in almost a disappointed whisper. He then regained his confidence. "Move up, yeah."

Rachel began to move up his peck to his neck. She was taking her sweet time, though.

"Just a little quicker," Frankie said as he saw Rachel move up to James' ear. "Yeah, right there, hold for a sec."

Rachel held there, sucking on James' earlobe. She sold it. She made it look like it was the most pleasurable thing that a woman could do to a man.

"Good... Good," Frankie said as he watched on, waiting for the "great" moment.

The "great" moment came when she stuck her tongue out and circled it around his ear.

"Great!" Frankie shouted, as though he was surprised. "Now cut there. Cut there!" He rose from his chair. "Tell me we fucking got that?"

No one seemed to let Frankie know if they got the shot he felt was there.

"Jesus Christ," Frankie said as he put his head in his hands. "Please tell me we fucking got that guys!"

"Hey, Frankie," Miles said as he walked up to Frankie. It was apparent Miles wasn't going to bring him good news.

"What, Miles?" Frankie said, not bringing his head up from his hands.

"Tony says we can't use this," Miles said, with the kind of fake disappointment that only Miles can muster.

"What?" Frankie said, sitting up in his chair. "Bring him here."

Miles walked off as Frankie threw his cigarette away and lit up another. He leaned back and looked up to the garage ceiling, hoping against hope that all of the bullshit would just go away.

"What's up, Mr. Wood?" Frankie heard the voice and recognized it instantaneously. It was the voice that pretty much woke him up that morning, without a doubt. It was also the voice of his "Director of Photography", which was a man he had met a million times before. Yet, his voice wasn't something he could pull from a line up.

"So why can't we use any of this shit?" Frankie asked, not letting on that his oh-so-trusted cinematographer was but just another face in the crowd to him.

"You were talking through it, Mr. Wood," Tony said matter-of-factly. "The sound is all fucked up."

"Can't we just fix it in post like we always do?" Frankie asked.

"Post?" Tony asked. It was as though he hadn't ever heard the term before.

"*Post-production*," Frankie said. He wanted to make fun of Tony's accent, just to accentuate the point that he believed Tony was a worthless piece-of-shit, but he didn't. He held his tongue. It would seem that Frankie still had some semblance of couth under the day-old Hawaiian shirt and grown-out blonde hair (not to mention the caterpillar mustache).

"What's that?" Tony asked, in all seriousness.

"Huh?" Frankie asked. He couldn't believe his ears. "Seriously?"

"What?" Tony was clearly unsure of how to answer. "Yes?" he finally chose.

"You fucking amateur," Frankie said as he stood up and walked off. It was clear he could no longer be bothered.

"Sir?" Tony asked after him, confused as confused could be.

"Amateur!" Frankie shouted at Tony, before he turned to face the rest of the crew. "Amateurs! All of you! I mean, god damn it. Do you all really think that just because you all watch porn that you can fucking make it? Mother-fucking-Christ!"

Frankie then stormed off as far away from Tony as he could possibly get while still being in the garage. He made his way to the set. It was a piss-poor excuse for a dorm room and he stood right in the middle of it sizing it all up.

"I mean, are you guys looking at this fucking thing?"

Frankie asked as he motioned around. He went up to the walls and shook them. He went to the door and nearly pushed it over. He stomped his feet down on the carpet and it made a rather unpleasant noise.

"Are any of you paying attention to any of this shit?" Frankie then walked over to the hyper-pink couch that was the centerpiece of the little scene they were shooting. "Do you guys see how fucking pink this is? Doesn't that strike any of you as a fucking cliché? Seriously, guys, c'mon. Get your fucking shit together. All of this is sad. It's all so fucking sad. You think some guy wants to bust off to some pathetic excuse for smut? Have some fucking respect for yourselves!"

He looked around to the crew, as though he expected a response. None came however and so he just fumed. As he fumed he looked down on the floor and saw a script lying there. Without much thought he angrily went for it, picked it up, and marched it over to James.

"And you, you lovesick fuck," he said to James as he approached him. "What is this fucking garbage you're pushing, huh?"

"What?" asked James, defensively. He then noticed, as Frankie was standing in front of him, that his cock was still out and so he tucked it back into his jeans as nonchalantly as one can. "You okayed it, Frankie," he then said.

"I don't doubt that," Frankie said, throwing the script onto the floor. "But I was probably fucking high as shit! I mean, fuck. I had to be. I absolutely had to

22

be. And you know what, James? You would've fucking known that. Don't you dare think for one second that you didn't take advantage of me. Jesus-fucking-Christ. How else would I approve such a trite and cliché, piece-of-shit script?" Frankie kicked the script on the floor.

"I'm sorry, Frankie but-" James was clearly trying to keep a level head.

"Oh, *you're* sorry, huh?" Frankie said. "You're fucking sorry? No, mother-fucker, you don't know what sorry fucking is. You know how much money this has all wasted already? This is all your god-damn fault."

"It ain't my fault you're high all the time, Frankie," James said with the tone of somebody who was jabbing the final knife into Caesar's back.

When Frankie heard James' backtalk he had to take a step back. The mere insinuation that Frankie wasn't respected was enough to send Frankie into a full-blown eruption. What James said was a straight up affront. Frankie knew that, but he liked James, he really did. At least he thought he did. Most people he liked didn't talk back. James did. James needed to be taught a lesson and even though Frankie did really try to hold off the explosion, his mind wouldn't let him. James needed to know where he stood.

"FUCK YOU!" Frankie shouted at the top of his lungs. It echoed louder than anything else had ever bounced off the walls of the garage. His face was red. His hands, in fists, shook violently as though he was ready to throw a punch.

"Frankie, brother, I'm sorry. Fuck, man, I'm really

23

sorry." James' calm and collected demeanor went out the door as soon as he had heard that hard "FAH" sound begin to escape Frankie's lips. It was clear he knew he had overstepped his bounds.

Normally, that would be good enough for some people, but Frankie wasn't just "some people". He was Frankie Fucking Wood and he'd be damned if he'd let anyone off that easy.

"Of course, you're fucking sorry!" Frankie yelled. "You're a fucking cliché hack! You know we're losing money with this stupid, inane shit and you don't give a flying fuck! You know why you should give a fuck? Huh, James? You know why you should fucking care?"

"N-No," James said, taking a step back, away from Frankie.

"Because I god damn trusted you!" Frankie was positively livid, even though it was clear that James had learned his lesson some time ago. "And you know I trusted you! And you say things like '*It ain't my fault you get high*' and you wanna know what? It fucking is! It so fucking is, you piece-of- shit! You think I'd need to get high if this shit was a success? And you know why it isn't a success? 'Cause you keep bringing me the same ol' shit to work with. I mean, fuck me! I am so sick of working with the clichés you insist on trying to spoon feed to me. You're such a fucking hack and it's killing me."

James tried to avoid eye contact with Frankie. He moved his eyes to the side and looked off. He moved his eyes further and met the crew's collective gaze. He

24

tried to smile it off when he saw everyone staring at him and Frankie, but they could all see how full of shit he was.

"It's fucking killing me!" Frankie exclaimed as he reached down and picked up the script. He began to rip it into shreds. Each shred he pulled off was flung into James' face.

"Frankie, I think you should cool it," Miles said, walking up to the soon-to-be altercation.

"And you know what, James?" Frankie said, ignoring Miles completely and pointing a finger right into James' face.

"What, Frankie?" James asked, trying to play it cool but shitting himself internally.

"Big, black fucks like you are a tired cliché," Frankie said. "You are a dime a dozen. You're so fucking fired."

"What?" James responded in utter disbelief.

"No, Frankie, don't," Rachel suddenly chimed in. She had just been standing there, right next to James, as all of it had transpired.

"What was that, Rachel?" Frankie asked, turning sharply to face her. He looked her up and down. He sized her up. He made note of her tussled blonde hair and her smeared lipstick. She looked like some sort of bastardized clown and Frankie couldn't help but laugh a little.

"I don't think you should fire, James," Rachel said. She had dropped the accent but still sounded ridiculous. "We won't do it again."

"Oh, I know you won't, Rachel," said Frankie with

all the scorn he could muster. "You know why?"

"Why?" Rachel asked, falling right into Frankie's trap.

"Because southern sluts are fucking cliché too. Get the fuck off my set," Frankie said as he pointed to the door.

"Oh, come on Frankie," Miles said in a pleading manner.

Frankie didn't say anything though; all he did was extend his middle finger up to James. He then moved his bird-giving hand to Rachel's face then on to Miles'. He held it in front of Miles' face for an uncomfortably long amount of time as he stared Miles dead in the eyes.

Miles just looked back and tried to beg Frankie to let Rachel and James stay with his eyes. It was clearly of no use.

"I'm fucking serious," Frankie said, turning to James and Rachel. "Why the hell are you guys still here?"

"Don't be serious," Miles said.

"I'll be whatever the fuck I want, Miles!" Frankie shouted, finally bringing the middle finger down. "Get them the fuck out of here. This *movie* is done."

"You can't just fire us!" Rachel shouted.

"Oh, is that so?" Frankie said, laying the sarcasm on thick. "Hey, Miles?"

"What, Frankie?" Miles said, obviously feeling more and more uncomfortable by the minute.

"Who, out of everyone here, can do whatever the fuck they want?" Frankie asked Miles with a very serious look on his face.

"Don't do this," Miles said. He sounded sterner than he usually did.

"You fucking answer me when I ask you a question," Frankie said to Miles more sternly than Miles could ever muster. "Unless you want to be next on the chopping block."

"You're the only one here that can do whatever he wants, Frankie," said Miles as though he'd rehearsed saying those words hundreds of thousands of times.

"Exactly," said Frankie as he turned back to Rachel. "So you're fired and so is James. This fucking movie is done. We're done. Fuck all this!" Frankie then turned to Miles, "Was I clear enough?"

"Yes, you were," Miles said with a slight hint of chagrin.

"Good," Frankie said before he turned to the rest of the crew. "Now tear this fucker down! I want this set gone come morning!"

With that, Frankie stormed off the set.

Rachel let out a sob. He could hear that it was a fake sounding sob, though, and so Frankie paid it no mind as he walked off.

Frankie then made it to the door that led into his home and turned to face the crowd. He held himself in a manner that befit Hitler, Stalin, or Nixon, and went to address them.

"All of you," Frankie began. "Leave me the fuck alone."

With that, he went inside and let the door slam behind him. After the door was closed he could have sworn that he heard James say something along the lines of "Fuck that guy," and Rachel sobbing louder and more dramatically. He paid it no mind, though. He just went back upstairs to his room and made his way into his bathroom as quickly as he possibly could.

As soon as he was in there, he couldn't help but take note (true note) of what a wicked mess the bathroom was. Had he really come so far as to let the place where he shit turn into the equivalent of a dive bar's restroom? It was for all intents and purposes, a drug din.

Now that he hadn't just woken up, he could really take the place in. There were little baggies of who-knows-what strewn across the place. Most of them had to be coke, but he happened across a little baggy that contained a brown, mushy lump. It looked like a little seed, but he knew what it really was. It had to be heroin.

"Fuck it," he said as he looked at the little baggy. "Why not?"

With that amount of conviction, he pulled out a twenty-dollar bill from his pocket and placed the little lumpy seed into it. He folded the bill and then moved the lump into the center of the fold. A lighter was then produced from his pocket and he began to heat the dollar bill where the "seed" was located, careful to not let the flame touch the dollar itself.

It took longer than expected.

Frankie figured, as he was waiting, that all of this might transpire quicker if he had some weed in him. He looked around the room and found a half-smoked joint

28

near the sink. He lit the fucker up and went back to the heroin in the dollar bill.

As Frankie had figured, the pot in his system seemed to make the H cook faster. He felt the lump and saw that it was drier than it had been previously. It wasn't to perfection, but at that point, he didn't care. He placed the little seed on a small picture frame that was coated in white powder.

Quickly (as though he had done it a million times before) he pulled out his Catchpenny's Rewards Card and began to cut up the heroin as best he could. The brown lump was still a little sticky. He knew he couldn't get through it under his current mellow mindset.

That's when he decided to do some bumps out of one of the other baggies strewn across the bathroom.

He had flashbacks to the night before. He remembered throwing the baggies around, as Rachel lay on the floor before him, butt-naked and spread-eagle. She had told him to make it rain, and he did. He threw each baggy down on top of her like it was cash and she giggled.

How could he not have known that her and James were an item?

Honestly, he felt like a little bit of an asshole. He wouldn't have brought Rachel up and done copious amounts of drugs with her as she tried to blow him and he tried to eat her out (both fruitless attempts) if he knew. It was just kind of a habit between them. He never thought anything of it. But, he knew now, after seeing them try to do the scene they were so proud of, that they had to be in love.

Is that why he fired James? Well, he fired James because James had been writing the shittiest shit imaginable for quite some time, but had the icing on the cake been when he came to the realization that James and Rachel were an actual item? Is that what drove him to pull the trigger (so to speak)?

*That can't be the case,* Frankie thought as he did a bump of what he hoped was cocaine and not meth, *I don't actually care about Rachel. I mean, I find her sexy, sure, but she'd not Maxine.*

Oh, how quickly it seemed that Frankie's mind would turn to Maxine.

He wouldn't allow himself to think about her, though. He knew he couldn't. He knew if he did he would be asking for an unenjoyable high. The last thing he wanted right now was an unenjoyable high. He just wanted to have a good time.

With that in mind, he probably did more of what he hoped was blow than he should have. It didn't take him long to realize that he was clenching his teeth with such force that it began to cause him pain. With that pain came remembrance, however.

He remembered he needed to get back to the precious heroin.

Frankie had been right when he had assumed that cocaine would help him cut through the H with more ease. It was like butter now. He was able to get it into little chunks and he was able to get those chunks to turn into some sort of powder-like substance. It was more sticky than powder, but it would do the job.

He then rolled the bill he had used to cook the heroin with into a nice little straw and snorted the brown up his nose.

The high he had hoped to feel was not instantaneous and so he did some more. And then some more. And some more after that. Soon, he'd done the whole little lump and he found that he was standing there in the middle of his bathroom feeling absolutely nothing.

It wasn't the good kind of nothing. It wasn't the nothing he was searching for. It was the nothing that meant nothing. It was the same vacantness he'd always felt.

It made him feel horrible.

He knew he needed to remedy it and so he dug around his bathroom. He found more baggies. Some were clearly crystal, but others could have been anything. He decided to taste and to choose. The substances that numbed his mouth, he did more of, the others he threw to the wayside to save for later.

It wasn't until it was far too late that he realized he had made a mistake.

He stood up, from the floor now littered with baggies and looked at himself in the mirror. It's then he saw it. The "it" being himself. When had he become an "it"?

There was nothing human about what he saw when he looked at himself in the mirror. It was just a mass of nothing but deep, dark shit wrapped up in a Hawaiian shirt with bleach blonde hair and a mustache that left much to be desired.

"How did I get here?" he asked the mass in the mirror.

The mass had no answer.

"How the fuck did I get here?" he asked again, hoping that the emphasis on the profanity would coax the mass to answer him.

It did not. It just stood there and stared back at him.

"Fuck," Frankie said as he turned away from the mirror. "How the fuck did I get here?" he then asked himself.

Himself acted in the same way as the mass, it had no answers to give. That depressed Frankie and he let himself sink to the floor.

"How did I get here?!" He shouted out to no one and no one answered back.

Frankie then closed his eyes for what would feel like a very long time.

# THE 2<sup>ND</sup> ACT OF
# THE GREATEST PORNO EVER MADE

His name was Francis Collinwood and he enjoyed skateboarding. That is to say, he didn't enjoy doing tricks on a skateboard (he wasn't a showboat); he just liked the act of riding one. He liked the ability to push and move and push and move and then flow. There was something especially therapeutic about it. His actions had results when he was on the board and he liked that. Maybe it was a control thing.

Either way, Francis took the board wherever he went and that day was no different. Currently, he was riding his board through a particularly suburban neighborhood, on the way to his girlfriend's house.

She was, what one might describe, as upper-middle class. That means that, to Francis, she was rich but to herself, she was poor. It was a strange thing that Francis had picked up on, but he loved her and so he didn't much think to bring it up.

On the other hand, he was, what one might describe, as

lower-middle class. That meant, to Francis, that he was poor, but to everyone else he wasn't poor *enough*. His family could afford bread and shit like that, they weren't food-banking it on the regular and he could afford a video camera and a skateboard.

Man, he loved that skateboard. It was probably the second most important thing he'd ever known. The first, of course, was his girlfriend, but the second had to be his skateboard.

That being said, the video camera (or, camcorder as it was more colloquially known at the time) was moving up in the ranks. It had belonged to his grandparents. They had spent quite a bit of their retirement money on it. It was apparently something they needed so that they could record all of their precious memories. Those memories they recorded couldn't be taken to the grave, though, as was apparent when they died and left the camcorder and all the tapes to Francis.

Francis took it with honor. He wasn't going to use it like they did. He wasn't going to squander its use on capturing that, which was happening; he was going to make things happen with it. He was going to be a filmmaker.

The camcorder could be a tool. It could be used to force situations to transpire and he could capture them on film (or tape, as it were).

Once he'd received it he began to write little scripts and things. He would concoct ideas and he would get everyone he knew together so that he could film these ideas. It, to him at least, was working like gangbusters.

34

Every idea he had come up with was working its way onto tape with the slightest of ease. It was almost as though he was meant to do it.

If he was going to take his filmmaking career to the next level, though, he knew he was going to have to start seeing if he could capture other people's ideas on his camcorder too. The only problem was that he didn't really know anyone that could give him ideas. At least none that were worthy.

Thank god he met his girlfriend, though. She was the beacon he had been searching for. She had ideas up the wazoo and wasn't afraid of sharing them.

In fact, that's where he found himself headed as he navigated the streets of suburbia, gliding on his skateboard. He was on his way to her, so they could film something they had been talking about for what felt like quite some time.

Eventually, after more difficulty than he thought was necessary, he found her house. It was a nice, two-storey house with an attached garage. To him it was a mansion, to her it was home.

He hopped off his board, picked it up and held it under his arm as he walked to the door. He knocked three times.

The door soon opened and there stood his girlfriend, Maxine Luna. He couldn't help but take in her beauty. Her wavy, brunette locks framed her face perfectly at that moment. Her hair was messy, to be sure, but there was something very sexy about it. It seemed as though it was mussed just-so, as though to give the illusion that she had just woken up, but he knew she hadn't. The two of them had spoken not an hour prior and she had said then that she had been up for awhile.

As he looked upon her, he couldn't help but feel as though all of the breaths he had ever breathed had been knocked out of his chest. She was, for lack of all the better words his mind couldn't conjure, beautiful.

"You doing alright?" Maxine asked with that should-be award-winning smile.

"Oh, yeah," Francis said back to her, "I'm just stunned by your beauty, as always." He paused for his half-joke to land and then carried on. "Did your parents leave?"

"Yes, sir-e," she said. Her dark skin seemed to radiate a deep orange aura of confidence.

"Great," he said, knowing full well that he sounded too excited.

"Did you bring the camera?" Maxine asked, clearly noticing that the conversation could take them to non-film realms very quickly.

"Of course," Francis said as he reached into his well-worn backpack and produced the camcorder.

"Good," Maxine said as she grabbed Francis by the shirt collar and pulled him into the house. "Let's get started." The look of seduction on her face was almost too much for Francis to take.

The next thing Francis knew, he and Maxine were kissing passionately and they were bursting into her room. Maxine stopped the kissing for a brief moment and took off her shirt. Francis took note of the fact that she wasn't wearing a bra.

He also took note of her breasts. They were like two

perfect mountains upon a plain of gorgeousness. The nipples, those wonderful nipples, sat atop them like two small satellite dishes with their feeds firmly transfixed on his eyes.

"What?" Maxine asked noticing Francis' staring. She was clearly trying to act insecure, but really she was just coming off as playful.

"Let me grab the camera," was all that Francis could think to say.

"Okay," Maxine said back. She then watched as Francis fumbled around in his backpack and pulled out the camera. "What do you want me to do?" she asked once she saw that the camera was aimed in her direction.

"Get on the bed," Francis said. To Maxine, that was the most serious he had ever sounded. It excited her.

As she was told to do, she got on the bed. She laid there, in a pose she found had been seductive in the past, and looked Francis dead in the eye.

"Take off your pants," Francis then said.

Maxine giggled a true giggle as she unbuttoned the button on her jeans. She then unzipped the zipper and slid out of them as seductively as one can when they are lying on their back on a bed. The pants were then thrown on the floor, near Francis, and she was all but bare. All that she had on was a lacy thong.

"Lose those panties," Francis said as he tried to line up the shot so it was perfect. He couldn't help but take note of how the little camera screen didn't do justice to Maxine's beauty. He hoped it would transfer over once the film was on a larger screen.

Again, she did as she was told. She took off her underwear and shot them, like a rubber band, towards Francis and the camera. It hit the camera dead on and she couldn't help but laugh.

Francis laughed too.

"That was awesome," he said before adding, "you are so fucking sexy."

"Turn off the light," Maxine said as she repositioned herself on the bed so that all that Francis could see was positively the most attractive thing he had ever known.

"But then how will I see your feet?" Francis half-joked. He wanted the camera to catch absolutely everything, but didn't want to say as much.

"Turn off the light," Maxine said, more seriously this time. To emphasize the seriousness, after she said what she said, she licked her fingers and placed them on her pussy. It was already plenty wet, but she wanted to make Francis think of her mouth when he thought of her cunt. Or vice versa, even.

She stuck her fingers inside of herself.

"What about the camera?" Francis asked, too caught up in what he was witnessing to be concerned with being coy any longer.

"You've got night vision on that thing, yeah?" Maxine asked as she fingered herself.

"But, Max…" Francis said, not knowing really how he'd argue with her. He was clearly at a loss for words, but he did want to capture everything that was about to happen on camera. Whatever was about to transpire was, without a doubt, worth recording.

Instead of arguing, Maxine moved her feet off the bed and began to rub them against Francis' hard cock through his jeans.

That was all that Francis needed to happen. He began to fiddle with the camera settings.

"Does that feel good?" Maxine asked.

"Yes, ma'am," Francis said as he turned off the lights and put the camera on night-vision. He approached Maxine with his camcorder in hand.

---

On the recording, it can be seen that in the darkness, Maxine covers herself with a playfulness that is almost too much for Francis to handle. She then unveils herself for the green-and-black recording to see. Maxine is just as attractive in this nearly alien light as she is in any other light. Her attractiveness seems to know no bounds.

With a swiftness that can barely be captured by Francis' camera-manning skills, she moves towards him and begins to undo his pants.

Before Francis knows what is happening, his dick has been pulled from his fly. It sits, firmly erect, in Maxine's hand. She closes her hand around it and begins to move it up and down, from shaft to head.

It's clear his dick is dry and so she spits on it. She doesn't spit like one spits when they're trying to rid their mouth of something unpleasant, instead she spits as though she intends to wet a surface with her salvia. She then let a little string of spittle hang from her mouth. It hung off her bottom lip and remained attached to his cock.

There was a small little rope that traversed the dark abyss between her green-lit face and his green-lit cock.

Maxine looks at the camera as she sucks up the spit, moving with it, so as not to break the rope, and put her lips on the head of his dick.

"Do you want this?" She asks, her lips hit the head of his cock as they move with each word.

"Yes," he says, trying to focus on the shot. He focuses more on her actions, though.

With his confirmation, she puts her lips on the tip of his head, as though she is about to kiss it. Instead she moves her head forward, letting her lips part as her mouth moves down his shaft. She works down it slowly and before long, she finds herself at the base of his shaft. She held there, without prompt, as though she knew it felt good.

Soon, however, she gags and removes her face from his crotch.

"You like when I gag on you?" Maxine asks the camera and, vicariously, Francis.

"Yes," Francis says. "Very much."

"Good," she says.

"Do it again," he commands. It is clear he is trying not to sound too eager, but nothing could keep his excitement hidden.

"No," Maxine says, coyly. "Now you watch me."

She then moves away from his dick and places herself in the center of the bed. She remains on all fours, but turns her ass to him so that the camera can get a good view of her goods.

Her ass looks positively perfect on camera. It is sweet and supple and round. All Francis wants to do is try and take a bite out of it. Each cheek looking like a firm piece of just-baked bread, but it can clearly be seen that there is meat in there. It flexes as she moves her legs to position herself better.

Maxine puts her head down on the bed and, again, licks her fingers. She moves her hand, around her back, and begins to part her lips. Her fore- and ring finger do the spreading while her middle finger plays around in between. She moans as she does this.

Francis watches with bated breath, through the camera, as she does this. He almost can't believe his eyes; it can be heard on the recording in the way he breathes. He'd been with Maxine sexually before, but what he was seeing happen was something he had only imagined in his wildest dreams. He honestly thought about pinching himself, but he didn't want to take his eyes off the wonderful spectacle he was beholding at the time.

Maxine, on the recording, then does something that is even more unexpected. She brings her fingers together, letting her vagina lips close the sweet hole Francis zoomed in on, and moved them upward, towards her ass-cheeks.

She then moves her legs further apart so that her cheeks separate just enough for Francis to see her asshole. Her fingers then move up to the area and began to circle the area. He watches as her middle finger (still glistening from her own juices) begins to circle her asshole. It moves around and around and around and seems to be pushing and pushing inward and then, without much notice, she puts her finger into her butt, up to the first knuckle. Maxine moans as this happened.

"Do you like my ass, baby?" she asks, in between moans of elation.

"Yes," Francis says, clearly sounding like he's holding something in.

"Then come here," Maxine says, "I want you to eat it."

"But-" Francis says, thinking that if he moves to eat out her ass then he would surely lose the shot.

"Just put the camera somewhere," Maxine says, reading his mind. "Set it so it looks good."

"Yeah," Francis says. At that moment it is clear that he honestly doesn't even know what he is saying; he just said the first word that popped into his head.

Soon, the camera is set on her desk, which was conveniently placed just close enough to her bed so that the camera could capture everything. The tableau is set as such: The bed is just able to be seen at the bottom of the frame; Maxine, in all her glory is positioned atop it, dead center in frame; other things can be seen in the room such as band posters and what not, but anyone watching the first time wouldn't have been able to pay any mind to them.

Francis, after he set the camera to capture that specific scene, moves to the bed and approaches Maxine. He forcefully removes her hand from her ass and sticks his face in between her cheeks. He kisses the in between sweetly before he begins to tongue the crack as a whole. He then moves his tongue around her asshole, trying to mimic the motions she had made with her fingers, before he sticks his tongue into her. He moves his tongue in and out as he brings his lips up to her skin and begins to suck, creating a certain kind of suction that, if Maxine's moans are to be believed, is pleasurable. He moves his hands across her feet and up her legs. They eventually make their way to her inner thigh and begin to play around with her pussy. It is wetter than the juiciest peach, and more open than a 7/11.

He plays around inside of her for quite some time before he can no longer help himself; he moves his hands from her cunt and goes for his dick.

"No!" she shouts. "Not yet!"

She then pushes his head away and rolls over. He is left there, staring at her, spread eagle. It is clear he doesn't know what to do. Half of him seems to want to put his lips on every part of her body that he could see in the sparse light, the other half wants to just penetrate her as quickly as possible.

"Eat me, you fool," she then says as she grabs him by his hair and forces his face into her vagina. "Eat me now!"

He does as he is told and begins to move his mouth and tongue around her pussy. When he watches the tapes later he would recall how it tasted like gone-bad strawberries and butter. It was the most delicious thing he had ever tasted. He got lost in it.

Some time passes before, Maxine re-grabs Francis' hair and pulls him up towards her.

He fights it, though.

It is clear that she wants his lips, wet with her moisture, on her lips but he wants to have fun with her body.

He moves up her slowly. He kisses her tummy. Her strong abs give him resistance as they tighten with amorous giggles, but still he kisses them as hard as he can. He works his way up to her naval and can't help but stick his tongue in her bellybutton. She laughs as he did this, and her laughter makes him harder. There is something supremely sexual about this innocuous act.

Francis doesn't linger there. He can sense that it makes her uncomfortable, and so he moves up. And up. And up. Before he really knows it he can feel his lips pushing against the flesh of her breasts.

He loves her tits. He wants them to know that and so he works his mouth up to her nipples and begins to suck. Within the suction he sticks his tongue out so that he can flick them with it. He loves her nipples, too.

Maxine loves having her nipples sucked, it can be heard as she moans out in pleasure as she feels Francis work them with his mouth. It is almost too much to take. Yet, it isn't enough. She wants more.

She grabs Francis' hair again and pulls his head up so that his mouth can finally meet hers.

The two of them make out for what feels like eternity. In filmmaking terms, it borders on dead air. It isn't a bad eternity, however, but a glorious one that both of them simultaneously wished would last forever and also wanted to end quickly so that the next, even more glorious, eternity could overtake them. They both knew what was about to come (no pun intended).

"Do it, Francis," Maxine says as she pulls Francis' head away from hers.

"But the condom," Francis says, trying to sound responsible.

"Not for the movie," Maxine said as she takes Francis' cock and puts it inside of her.

That is all that Francis needs to hear. All apprehensions he has, during the filming, about condomless sex went out the window and he thrusts himself into Maxine with more force than he ever thought he could conjure.

As he humps within her, his hands move about her body. They feel every crevice she has to offer. They start at her face and hold it as he kisses her, but soon they move down her throat. One hand stays on her throat, she holds it there, and his thumb moves along the muscles of it. He can feel them quiver and pulse with each thrust and moan.

His other hand moves down, along her collarbone. It grips her shoulder for a moment, before he let's it loose and places his body on top of hers. The hand then moves around down to her armpit, and then around to her back. He feels her shoulder blade move as she grips his ass and forces a rhythm that is more her speed.

Before he knows it, his hand moves around to her front side. It is placed upon her breast and it grips it tightly. He moves his face down to meet it and takes her nipple in his mouth.

Once his hand is sure that his mouth can take over where it left off, it moves down the rest of her body. It moves back to her back. It inches its way down her lower spine and eventually makes it to her ass.

He clenches it like it was a buoy keeping him a-float,

although, ironically his grip, and the feeling of her ass cheek in his hand seemed to submerge him further into the euphoria that would make him climax.

Climaxing like this is not what he wants, though.

With that thought in mind he flips her over. He wants to take her from behind. There is something very animalistic about this action.

Francis thrusts into her with much more force than he had been using previously. The image of her on her stomach, all but helpless, really does something for him.

Maxine moans out in elation. It is clear that she loves the position switch as much as he does.

He moves his hand back to her throat, this time from behind. He held it fiercely and tightens each grip with each thrust he gives.

She moves her feet up. Her knees bend and she positions her feet between herself and Francis. The tops of her feet rub against his stomach. She knows he likes looking at her soles and so she shows them to him and to the camera as well. Her hands move up, across the back of her body, before they clasped themselves around her ankles, so that she can hold her feet in place.

This is too much for Francis to take.

"I'm going to cum," he says, each syllable almost broken by his thrusts.

"Good," Maxine says.

"Tell me where to cum," Francis demands between gasps for air. It is apparent that this is something he has never said before. What he meant was "Should I cum inside you, because I want to, but don't want to get you

46

pregnant" but he thought that if he worded it that way it would be way less sexier.

"My face," Maxine says, her face half-covered by her hair, pushed into the bedding. It comes out unintelligible.

"What?" Francis asks, rushed. He needs to know where to do his business quickly.

"Cum on my face," Maxine shouts as she turns her face from the sheet on the bed. "I want you to cum on my fucking face!"

"Okay," Francis says as he thrust harder into her.

"But on camera," she adds.

"What?" He asks, too close to ejaculation to be able to comprehend what she just said.

"Get it on camera," Maxine says as she moves away from Francis so that his member just hangs there, in the air, so hard it's throbbing.

"Alright," Francis says, understanding what she wants but knowing they don't have long. "Let's go."

The two of them then move off the bed and make their way, quickly, angling themselves closer to the camera in a way that showcases Maxine's soon to be cum-painted face.

Francis then puts his hand around his dick and strokes it.

Maxine moves her head to just below his cock's head and sticks out her tongue.

"Cum on my face, baby," she says in almost a whisper.

And as though Maxine willed it, Francis releases his load onto her. She takes it laughing.

It isn't an impressive load; by any means, but the first spurt make it up to her left eye, which she closes abruptly.

The rest comes out around her mouth and her chin. There is a particularly attractive squirt that hangs off her chin.

He looks down at her and can't help but realize that this was the most ejaculate he has ever produced. He says something about it, but it can't be fully heard on the recording. It isn't a lot, he knows, but it is enough to make her face look sexier than he'd ever seen it.

"Fuck, that was a big load," Maxine says, it is unclear if she heard what Francis said about it or not.

Francis can't tell, either. She might be playing it up for the camera, but the way she says it sounds genuine.

"I love you, Maxine," Francis says to her. It is clear through tone; he means it when he says it.

Maxine doesn't answer, at first. What she does instead is wipe up his cum with her fingers and sucks it into her mouth. It takes more than one attempt, and she laughs as she does each swipe. She moves her finger around her face and then circles them around each glob she comes across. Once it is on her finger, she puts it into her mouth and sucks the cum off. She does this over and over and over again. She can't help but look glamorous as she does this.

"I love you too, Francis," she says after she's haphazardly wipes all the cum up and eats it.

The two of them then look at each other and share what can only be described as "a moment".

"I think we should turn off the camera," Maxine says after the moment passes.

He then can be seen nodding and turning the camera off. The screen goes black.

When Francis and Maxine woke up the next morning they couldn't help but watch the film they had shot the night before.

"I think we need to do some reshoots," Maxine said after watching it the first time through.

"What?" Francis asked as he rewound the footage, so they could watch it again. "You're crazy."

"No," Maxine said, as she looked at Francis, "I just think we can redo some of the stuff we did from different angles."

"Maybe," Francis said reluctantly, he then found a good place to stop rewinding. "But look at this."

"What about it?" Maxine asked as she looked at the freeze-framed image of her bending over that Francis had stopped on.

"I think this is my favorite bit," Francis said with a smile on his face, "I mean, look at how sexy you look."

"I do look pretty sexy," Maxine agreed. "Look at my ass. I have a nice ass."

"You think I can look at anything other than your ass?" Francis laughed as he said that. "I mean even in jeans it's a pretty slamming ass."

"'*Slamming ass*?' Really?" Maxine always had to make fun of him.

"Isn't that what the kids are saying nowadays?" Francis thought it was funny to act like an old man.

"Yeah, yeah," Maxine said, playing it off. "But, look, fast forward a bit."

Francis did as he was told and pushed the double-arrow button on his camcorder.

"Stop," Maxine said.

Francis pushed the pause button.

"See there," Maxine said as she pointed to the little monitor that jutted off the camera. It showed a rather unflattering image of Maxine as she was repositioning herself the night before. Her stomach rolled and her face looked like she was constipated and sneezing. "You see that there? That looks gross."

"Oh, c'mon," Francis said, clearly not seeing what Maxine was seeing, "I think you look good."

"Psh," Maxine said, "you always think I look good."

"I can't help it if I'm in love with you, babe," Francis said with a shrug before he pressed play on the camcorder again. "Let's watch it again."

"No, no, no," said Maxine. "If we see it again I might take the tape and burn the fucker."

"Oh come on, now," Francis said, moving the camcorder away from her instinctually. "You can't take it away from me. It's my birthday present, remember?"

"Yeah, but there'll be more birthdays, won't there?" Maxine asked. The way in which she said it was, in her mind, to make light of the situation, but it would appear as though Francis didn't pick up on it.

"Yeah, but still," Francis said genuinely. "This is my first birthday with you and I'll be damned if you take this tape from me." He then laughed. "You'll have to pry it from my cold, dead hands."

"I know, I know," Maxine said with her signature smirk, "I won't take it. I want to though."

"I know you do," said Francis. "I don't know why, I

really like it. I think it's the hottest thing ever caught on film."

"You really like it?" Maxine non-jokingly asked. She dropped her nonchalant demeanor for something more sincere.

"Of course I do," Francis said, meeting her sincerity. "It is very, very sexy baby."

"That's good," she said, rolling away from him. "Because I was thinking maybe we could make a thing out of it." She turned her head around so that she could catch a glimpse of him in her peripheral.

"What do you mean by 'a thing'?" Francis asked, still fiddling with his camcorder. "Like do you mean we do this again?"

"Oh," Maxine said, turning back to face him, "did you think I was kidding about reshoots?"

"Well yeah," Francis said, in all seriousness, "I can never tell when you're joking or not."

"Well I wasn't joking about that," Maxine said. "Reshoots are necessary."

"But we can shoot other things too?" Francis asked as he took his gaze away from the camcorder's little monitor.

"Yeah, of course," Maxine said matter-of-factly. "It makes me feel sexy. I like feeling sexy."

"I would like if we did that," Francis said, looking at her with puppy dog eyes. "Very much."

"You want to do it now?" Maxine asked with a sparkle in her eyes.

"Now-now?" Francis asked.

"Now-now," Maxine confirmed.

She then moved in to kiss him and as they kissed, she could see Francis fumbling with the camera trying to set it to record.

"Here let me see it," Maxine said after she felt Francis had fumbled with the camcorder long enough.

She took it from his hands and deftly moved it from the playback position to the recording position.

"Let's do this," Maxine said as she got up and put the camera on the desk where it had been the night before.

"Where do you want me?" Francis asked as she set up the angle.

"I was just about to ask you the same thing," she said as she walked back over to the bed and put his cock in her mouth.

---

The majority of Francis and Maxine's relationship could be summed up in the videos they recorded.

The second time they recorded themselves making love (not including the reshoots), Francis takes her from behind and puts pressure on her asshole with his thumb as he fucks her and she moans. It can be seen in the recording that the two of them are very passionate towards one another. Maxine keeps looking over her shoulder to Francis and the two of them kiss occasionally. Maxine requests that Francis cum "all over" her. He does and "I love you's" are exchanged.

The third time they recorded themselves having sex, Maxine sits on Francis' lap as he sits in a chair. He pulls her hair and touches her breast. They both say "I love you" before climax has been reached. Maxine begs Francis to cum inside of her, which he eventually does. They kiss passionately afterward.

The fourth time they recorded themselves fucking, Francis stands at the edge of the bed and plows into Maxine. He holds her legs up, at her ankles, as she lies on her back. This is the most physical contact that one can see in the video. "I love you," is not said once within the video and when Francis asks if he can cum inside of her. Maxine says, "Not today". So Francis cums haphazardly on her stomach.

The fifth recording shows Francis holding Maxine upside down. He legs are wrapped around his head and he is eating out her pussy as she sucks his cock. No words are exchanged and Francis just cums, without any warning, as he stops licking Maxine and holds her head as her mouth is wrapped around his cock. She takes it like a champ, but it is clear she is not expecting it and is not happy with the outcome.

The sixth time they recorded began with Maxine telling Francis that he needs to let her know when he is going to cum. She then takes him in her mouth and sucks and sucks until he cums, not warning her. She receives nothing in return and it is evident that she doesn't like this. It is brought up in the recording, but the video is cut short once the fight begins to ensue.

The final recording of the two of them is a short affair. It is less than five minutes long and all it involves is Maxine laying in bed, on her stomach, her hair wet from a shower as though she has somewhere to be, and Francis coming over to her and fucking her from behind. He humps away at her. Maxine lets out soft moans, but nothing substantial. It is as though she isn't into it (and is she into faking it either).

"Where do you want me to cum?" Francis asks in this recording.

"On my ass I guess," Maxine says, trying to sound sexy but coming across as though she can't be bothered.

He cums on her ass, kisses her on the forehead, and gets up to turn off the camera.

They recorded no more videos after that.

# THE 3<sup>RD</sup> ACT OF
# THE GREATEST PORNO EVER MADE

His name was Francis Collinwood and he sat at a table in the nicest restaurant he had ever been in. It was the kind of place that didn't put prices on the menu. He didn't know how to order from a place like that. He usually went for the cheapest thing, but here he couldn't do that. Price didn't matter, though. He was here to celebrate his anniversary with the girl he adored the most.

Maxine Luna, his girlfriend, sat across from him. She looked very unhappy, but Francis was oblivious to that fact.

He had no idea that his heart was about to be broken.

"I don't think this is working out, Francis," Maxine said as she looked at him with sorrow in her eyes. Immediately after she spoke she took a large drink of water.

"What?" Francis asked, not believing his ears. Of all the things Maxine could have said, that was the furthest from the possibilities he could have predicted. Why had she agreed to come to the nice restaurant with him if that's what she was going to say?

"I can't keep doing this," Maxine said as she put her empty water glass back on the table.

"Why not?" Francis asked, clearly befuddled by all that was transpiring, "I thought everything has been going great."

"Well," Maxine said with a shrug. "It's not."

"You just asked me to move in with you," Francis said as he recalled how, not a month prior, Maxine had said that it might be best if the two of them got an apartment together.

"I know," Maxine said, clearly feeling shame about having asked Francis, "I just changed my mind, though."

"But I packed up all my shit, Maxine," Francis said, trying to not lose his cool in this very fancy and public place. "It's all literally in my car outside right now."

"Sorry," Maxine said, clearly surprised by this news, "I didn't know."

"Well of course you didn't fucking know," Francis said, catching himself before he could raise his voice, "I was going to surprise you with it."

"Well," Maxine said, trying to think on her feet. "Couldn't you take it all back?"

"What? No! I can't take it all fucking back, Maxine," Francis was, despite his best efforts, losing his cool. "I told my dad to go fuck himself when I left. You can't seriously think I can go back to his house after I did that?"

"Well I never asked you to do that, Francis," Maxine said as though she hadn't.

That is to say, she really *hadn't*, but it had been *implied*. She knew what kind of relationship Francis had with his father. The two of them butted heads constantly. Francis' father thought that Francis was wasting his life and in his father's defense, Francis thought he was right. Perhaps that's why they fought so much.

None of that mattered now, though. All that mattered was that Francis had packed up all of his shit, told his father to go fuck himself, and put it all in his car. He had been convinced that he was going to start a new life. She had convinced him. She had put that thought in his head. He had thought he was safe. He was sure she'd take him in for a bit and then they'd find a place together.

"I know you didn't ask me to," Francis said, after he gave her statement some thought. "But you made me think I could."

All Maxine could do at that moment was look at Francis. It was clear that she genuinely felt bad for him.

"What?" Francis asked, not because he couldn't see what she was thinking, but because he wanted her to say something. Anything, really.

"I'm sorry, Francis," Maxine said, really feeling it, "I really am."

"I just…" Francis said before he had really been able to wrap his mind around all that was happening, "I just don't understand where this is coming from. I mean, what is it? Where is this fucking coming from?"

"Please don't make a scene," Maxine said, as she looked around, slightly anxious of who might be drawn in by his raising voice.

"I'm not making a scene," Francis said, defending himself, "I just feel like I have a right to know where this is coming from."

"I just realized that I don't want to live with you anymore," Maxine said, point blank.

"Why not?" Francis asked, not finding her answer satisfactory.

"It just dawned on me," Maxine said, again looking around as though people might be listening to them, "that if you lived with me, we'd probably have to bone a lot."

"What's wrong with boning a lot?" Francis asked, raising his voice to a point he knew was too loud. Honestly, at that moment, he didn't care. "I thought you liked boning."

"I did," Maxine said. "But I don't anymore. It just makes me feel cheap and used now. Like you don't even respect me, you're just using me to get off. It's the only thing we do now when we see each other and it just makes me sad whenever it happens."

"But-" Francis tried to start, but he was cut off by Maxine.

"No don't," she said. "There's nothing you can say. I've made up my mind."

Francis just stared at her. He tried to think of what he could possibly say to undo the mess he'd made, but he kept coming up short. Maybe she was right. She couldn't be right, though. That would mean the end of them. He didn't want them to be over. He wasn't prepared to live without her.

"I'm sorry, Francis," Maxine said after Francis

remained silent for quite some time, "I think I should go."

With that statement, Maxine stood up and looked down at Francis. He looked back at her with the saddest eyes he had ever looked out of.

"What am I supposed to do?" Francis asked, feeling void of all hope.

"You'll figure something out," Maxine said as she grabbed her coat off the back of the chair. "You're a resourceful guy."

She then leaned in and kissed him on the cheek, one last time. He felt her lips' touch resonate throughout him.

"I will always love you, Francis," Maxine said as she began to walk away.

"Then stay with me," Francis pleaded.

"No," Maxine said, "I can't anymore. I respect myself to much." She then walked away completely.

"Well if you love me then why are you leaving me?" He called after her.

She didn't hear it, though. Or if she did, she didn't turn around or acknowledge it in anyway.

"Why the fuck are you leaving me, then?!" Francis repeated in a louder tone. He could tell that everyone in the restaurant was staring, but he didn't care.

Maxine left the restaurant then and Francis found himself sitting there, all alone.

"FUCK!" he shouted, "FUCK, FUCK, FUCK!" He slammed his fists on the table before he calmed down a bit. "Well fuck me then."

He then paid the check and left the restaurant too. He didn't take any of the food to go.

After the whole ordeal that had just transpired, he sat in his car and had what some would call a nervous breakdown. He looked around at the boxes of shit he'd shoved into his car and began to cry. What was he going to do? He wracked his brain trying to think. Nothing came to mind.

He thought about driving to Maxine's and trying to beg her to take him back, but by that point, he was feeling way too embarrassed to do that. She had made a fool out of him once that night already, he couldn't let it happen again.

Francis knew she was right, or at least she thought she was right, about their relationship. If he were honest he could admit that he had just gotten to a weird point in their relationship where he really had just been using her to get off. But what the fuck were relationships for, if not that? Was it really his fault that she didn't ask for reciprocation? He would've eaten her out. He would have fingered her until she came. Fuck, if she had really been more vocal about sex, he would have kept going until she came. It had always just been when he was done they were done. It takes two to tango.

"Fuck," he said to himself in his car as he thought about all of it. "Fuck, fuck, fuck." He looked around his car and then out into the street. "What the fuck am I going to do?"

He thought further about the question he asked himself. He *really* thought about it. He knew his options were limited. Very limited. He was afraid he would have to go back home.

Francis would be damned if he went back home, though. He'd burned that bridge and he didn't want to go back. He could live in his car. Or couch surf. Homelessness seemed like a better option.

"Yeah!" he said to himself when he thought about it, "I can fucking couch surf."

He ran down the list of people he knew in his mind. He went through his phone. He weighed pros. He weighed cons. He thought of people he was still cool with and people he wasn't. He hadn't talked to most people in a long time. He knew surely someone wouldn't mind a call out of the blue from him. Only one name seemed like it would suffice:

Miles Johnson.

---

Francis walked up the stairwell to Miles' apartment and was glad Miles had answered his call. If he hadn't then Francis would most assuredly be fucked beyond belief. He had nowhere else to go. Nowhere else he *wanted* to go, at any rate.

He knocked on Miles' door and Miles answered promptly.

"Hey, man," Miles said as though it hadn't been ages since they'd seen each other, "I was worried you got lost."

"I did a little bit," Francis said with a laugh. "This place is kind of hard to find."

"Yeah," Miles said, "I kind of like it that way."

Francis didn't know what to say to that, instead he just sort of chuckled and stared at Miles.

"You should come in, man," Miles said as he moved aside and motioned for Francis to come inside.

"Thanks for doing this for me," Francis said as he entered the modest apartment. "I know it has been awhile."

"Oh, no worries man," Miles said as he closed the door and turned to face Francis. "It has been awhile, though, hasn't it?"

"Yeah," said Francis.

"Well there's not a better way to catch up on lost time, huh?" Miles said with a smirk, he then walked into the living area, which was mere feet from the door.

"Yeah, that's a good point," Francis said, following him into the shabby, little place.

"So," said Miles, motioning to the couch. "You can sleep here, there's a foldout inside of it. It's not overly comfortable, but it's better than the couch."

"Thanks man," Francis said as he set his backpack down. "You're a lifesaver."

"Don't mention it," Miles said. He then motioned to an old desktop computer sitting on a crappy desk. "Feel free to use that computer, man. You know to look for places or jobs or whatever. I've got one in my room, so that one's all you."

"Sweet, man, thanks," Francis said.

"No problem," Miles said as he just stood there, staring at Francis.

Francis began to feel a little uncomfortable, he knew he hadn't seen Miles in awhile, but Miles seemed to be acting a little strange.

"What?" Francis asked, concerned, before he turned it into a joke. "Do I have something on my face?"

"Nah, man," Miles said with a laugh, "I'm just waiting for you to spill the beans on what happened. I mean, I know we haven't seen each other in awhile, but I knew you and Maxine and you guys seemed pretty solid. I mean, at least on the outside or whatever."

"I don't know what to tell you man," Francis said with a shrug. "She broke up with me."

"Well yeah, no shit," Miles said with a laugh. "But like why?"

"I'd rather not talk about it right now," Francis said, "I mean it just happened, you know? I'm still trying to process shit."

"Yeah," Miles said, "I feel that. That's cool, that's cool." He then looked around the room awkwardly for a moment before he turned back to Francis. "You all set here?"

"Yeah man, I'm good," Francis said as he looked around the cramped apartment. "All this is perfect, thanks again."

"Man, seriously don't sweat it," Miles said. "Do you want a beer or something?"

"Nah, I'm okay," Francis said, "I don't drink."

"Oh yeah, that's right," Miles said. "Sorry, I forgot."

"Oh, it's cool," Francis said before he joked, "I might pick it up."

"Well if you do, the kitchen is all yours," Miles said as he made his way to his bedroom. "And, seriously man, you can stay here as long as you want. If you're here longer than a month, though, I'm going to need some help with rent."

"Of course," Francis said, "I'll figure something out at some point."

"Cool, man," Miles said as he went into his bedroom. "Goodnight. Let me know if you need anything."

"Will do," Francis said. "Goodnight."

Miles closed his bedroom door and Francis found himself left to his own devices. He looked around the place and took notice of how dingy it seemed. It was the quintessential bachelor pad: a couch, a computer, and a kitchen with sparsely anything in it. Honestly, to Francis, it was a nice change of pace.

He made his way to the fridge and opened it up to check out what was inside. There was fuck-all save for a few cans of beer.

Francis eyed the beer and thought about taking one. He hadn't had a drop of alcohol in over a few years. The last time he had drank, he acted like such a fool that he couldn't ever forgive himself for it. He had decided then and there (after he had woken up that next morning with the most severe hangover anyone could ever imagine) that he wasn't ever going to touch alcohol again.

He had issued a little caveat when he made that promise to himself, however. It was something he'd never told anyone. It was a secret he had kept to himself. He had said, that if he ever felt the need to drink, than of course he could.

Up until that moment in time, he had never felt the urge. Now that he was looking at the cans of beer in

Miles' fridge, he couldn't help but lick his lips with anticipation.

"Fuck it," Francis said as he grabbed a cold can from the refrigerator.

Before he knew it, he had cracked that one open and then had another and another. He was feeling pretty good. Better than good, actually.

Not as good as he could be feeling, though.

He looked at the computer and ideas started popping into his head. He went to it and turned it on. It made a sound as it booted up and he felt a little insecure that Miles would hear him. As soon as he was able, he turned the volume on the machine as far down as it would go.

Once the computer had booted up in full, he logged onto the internet and went to a search engine of his preference.

He sat there as the cursor blinked in the search bar and thought about what he was in the mood for.

If he were honest, he was only in the mood for Maxine. He briefly thought about going to the camcorder he had in his backpack and playing back the exploits he and her had shared. He knew that would only depress him, though. So he opted not to.

Francis turned his attention back to the search engine. He typed in one word:

**Feet**

He looked at the word after he typed it and thought about it. Would that be enough for him? Just feet?

Surely, he would need something else. Surely, he could find something else. He had the whole internet at his disposal.

He added a word to it:

**Feet cum**

*There*, he thought, *that's good enough.* But did he really want "good enough"? He could have the world. He knew deep down what he was looking for. He decided to just search for what his heart desired. There was nothing to lose.

He rephrased his search query:

**Babe licks cum off own feet**

It didn't get more precise than that. That was what he wanted to see and so that was what he would find.

He pressed enter.

The search engine took no time in producing result upon result for him to search through.

After much deliberation (and clicking on some dead links) he finally found a video that he thought would suffice. It wasn't quite what he was looking for but it was close.

When he had typed "Babe licks cum off own feet," into the search box, he had conjured the image of a lady, hopefully brunette, foot fucking some lucky, big-cocked stud until said stud came all over her pretty feet. She would then lick it off her toes and moan all the while.

That's what he had wanted. Or at least that's what he thought he wanted.

What he got, instead, was something quite spectacular. He was treated to a video, of the homemade variety, in which the lady had stretched her body in such a way so that her feet were right by her mouth, and in between them was a cock. The cock fucked the feet and the mouth at the same time. It was a rapid, almost jarring motion, and she made wonderful sucking and gagging sounds.

It was almost too much for Francis to bear. Just when he was about to relieve himself, something caught his eye and interrupted his whole thought process. He noticed the name of the site he was on:

**www.sluttyexgirlfriendskankhoes.com**

Something about it tugged at him, he couldn't quite put his finger on what it was. He sat there, holding his dick in his hand for quite some time, just thinking about what it could be. Honestly, it took longer than it should've but he hadn't drank in what felt like an eternity. Then, like a bolt from nowhere, it hit him what exactly it was about the website's name that resonated with him. It was the word "exgirlfriend".

As he came to that realization he looked over to his backpack and couldn't help but think about the camcorder and tapes that were enclosed within it.

An idea then struck him like a bolt of lightening.

Before he could fully comprehend what he was doing, he stood up, pulled up his pants, and walked to Miles' door. He knocked on it repeatedly until Miles opened it, he was wearing nothing but boxers.

"What the fuck, man?" Miles asked, half-awake and slightly worried.

"Sorry, I didn't mean to wake you up," Francis said.

"Have you been drinking?" Miles asked.

"Yeah," Francis said, "I felt like it."

"Well good for you," Miles said. "But do you know what fucking time it is?"

"I don't care, man," Francis said, "I just got the best idea ever."

"Okay," said Miles, his curiosity piqued, slightly.

"Can you still do stuff with computers?" Francis asked.

"What do you mean?" Miles was still clearly half-asleep.

"Can you still do stuff with computers?" Francis repeated. "Like with websites and stuff. Do you think you could make a website?"

"Sure," Miles said before he thought about it. "Probably. I don't know. What did you have in mind?"

"Well," Francis said as a large, devilish grin grew on his face, "how do you feel about getting into the pornography business?"

---

Two months later, Francis and Miles stared at the homepage to *frankiesgirlfriends.com*, while they smoked some pot, in Miles' living room. Francis hadn't moved out yet, but he had found a way to pay Miles' rent. It involved putting Maxine's videos on the web and charging people to watch them. He felt guilty about doing it (at first), but the copious amounts of booze and the weed helped him get over the guilt. Also, the thought of money enticed him. Really, though, he thought Maxine deserved it.

"I like this layout better than the last one you had," said Francis as he pointed to the "Frankie's Girlfriends" logo that Miles had come up with. "The logo looks great, too."

"Thanks, man," Miles said, "I do think this is the layout we should go with."

"I think so too," Francis agreed.

"It's perfect," Miles said. "You think we're ready to go live?"

"Yeah, let's do it," Francis said. "Do we just push a button or something? I don't know how this shit works."

"I'll take care of it," Miles said as he went to the computer and began to click-clack on the keyboard.

Francis smirked as he went over to the couch and grabbed Miles' bong. He lit it up and inhaled. The bubbling sound filled the room for a second before he slid the stem out and sucked the smoke into his lungs. He held it for a while and blew it out; the room was then caught in a cloud.

"Hey, man, how are we going to pay for this?" Miles asked, spinning around in his desk chair away from the computer.

"Won't it pay for itself?" Francis asked. All the weed was starting to get to him. He found he couldn't really think straight. He figured if he drank more it could help. He grabbed the vodka bottle they'd just picked up and poured some of it into the coffee mug he'd been drinking out of.

"Well yeah, eventually," Miles said. "But now we need a credit card."

"I don't have a credit card," Francis said. "It's hard to get one nowadays I think. I don't know. I can't recall if I've ever looked into it."

"I have one, man," Miles said, "but honestly I'm going a little broke."

"Do you think this idea's any good?" Francis asked as he added orange juice to his vodka. "Like do you think it's gonna make money?" He took a big gulp of his drink.

"Yeah," said Miles. "Doesn't porn always make money? And Maxine is hot. Also, if you really think you can set up more dates and do this some more, we might have an actual fucking business on our hands. I think you could make a few hundred thousand dollars easy."

"If you pay to put the site up," Francis said, finishing his vodka/orange juice and realizing his mouth felt dry. "You'll be like my partner. We'll split it all fifty-fifty."

"Alright," Miles said. "Deal."

Miles then went back to click-clacking away.

Francis sat there and looked at the ceiling of the apartment. He thought it was strange that the ceiling was smooth. All the ceilings he had ever known (or at least paid attention to) had that stuff on them that made them look coarse. Or was that walls? Was he thinking of walls?

"Hey, Miles…" Francis said, intending to ask him about the ceiling, but forgetting about it as soon as he began speaking. His mind drifted somewhere. He couldn't quite place where it went. It was on the cusp of an idea, a twinkle of a thought. He couldn't see it yet. For a moment, he felt like a fool. His heart started beating fast. He had to think of something to say or else he would look like an idiot. He hated looking like an idiot. He asked the first thing that popped into his head:

"Do you think I'm going to be able to pull in some chicks?"

"What?" Miles asked not looking away from the computer. "Pull them into what?"

"You know," Francis said, trying not to let his mind wander, to the fleeting idea, he thought it had something to do with his name. "Like, you think I'll be able to find dates?"

"Yeah, why not?" Miles asked, focusing more on what he was doing than the conversation. "You're a pretty attractive guy. I mean, not to sound faggy, but I'd do you." Miles then turned around and smiled a huge smile to accentuate his joke.

Francis laughed and poured some more vodka into his coffee mug. Miles went back to work.

"I don't know," Francis then said, "I just don't know. Like with Maxine, things were easy. Her and I just clicked. I guess I'm just nervous about having to try to force that "click," you know? I feel like this site could be good, but if I can't bring in more chicks, then it won't make money."

"I'm sure you'll pull it off," Miles said before he hit a key on the keyboard in an over-exaggerated fashion. "That's the end of that. We now have a porn site!"

"Awesome," said Francis as he grabbed another coffee

cup and began to pour vodka into it. He handed it to Miles. "This deserves a drink."

"Thanks," Miles said as he took the drink and sat on the couch.

"I don't know why I'm so nervous," Francis said, after he had thought about it, "I'm sure I'll be able to do it." He didn't sound convinced.

"Dude, Francis, you need to chill, alright? This insecurity shit will be the end of you. You're Francis Fucking Collinwood, you can do anything man. Just keep telling yourself that, okay?" Miles said in a caring manner.

"Yeah, you're probably right," Francis said as he thought about it, "but, you know, I don't think Francis is who I want to be anymore. You should probably start calling me Frankie…"

# THE 4<sup>TH</sup> ACT OF
# THE GREATEST PORNO EVER MADE

His name was Frankie Wood, but that wasn't the name he gave his date. To her he was Frank. Just Frank. Only Frank. He hated being called Frank, almost as much as he hated the restaurant he found himself in.

He had decided, after the third or fourth girl he'd been out with, that in order to be able to film them fucking, he was going to have to be driven by something. He decided that drive would be bringing back up the thoughts of Maxine breaking up with him. That's why he brought all of the dates he intended to shoot for *frankiesgirlfriends.com* to this place. They even sat at the same table.

Frankie looked over at his date. Her name was Rachel and she was blonde. She was nothing like Maxine. In fact she was pretty much the opposite. She had light skin, light hair and big tits. She was also overly flirtatious and most of the conversations they'd had tended to always lean towards something sexual in nature. She wore something slutty on every date they'd had, and he could tell she had a very good body and wasn't afraid to show it off.

He hadn't seen her naked yet, but he could tell that she wanted him too. It was only their third date. He liked drawing it out. He found that it was more exciting for him and that they were more willing to be filmed. Filming required trust and each date earned more and more trust. By the third of fourth date Frankie found that it was just enough time to talk them into it in such a way that they would think it was their idea.

That was the best part of all of it for him at that point. He had grown bored with the sex, with sucking on their nipples and toes, with smacking their ass or having their nails drawn down his back. He was even rather unenthused whenever he would climax and he'd bust off on her ass or tits or face. Frankie knew it was fun, but the real orgasm in all of it was filming these girls and putting it online to make money.

He found he had become a piece-of-shit.

He didn't care, though.

"…and then my boss told *me* to clean it up," Rachel was finishing up a rather long and dull story as she let out a little laugh. "Like it was *my* job or something. Can you believe it?"

"That's hilarious!" Frankie said, clearly feigning interest (he knew she wouldn't pick up on it, though). "What did you do?"

"Well I did it…" Rachel said, a little ashamed, as she looked down at her half-eaten *Boccone Dolce*, "I can't really afford to lose my job at the moment, you know?"

"Oh yeah," Frankie said trying to commiserate, but

having trouble relating to what she was talking about, "I hear the economy is bad now."

"Yep," said Rachel in that perky tone of hers, before she leaned in, a clear attempt at changing the subject. "So it dawned on me the other day that we've seen each other quite a bit this past week and I have no idea what you do for a living."

"Well what can I say?" Frankie said. "I'm not really much into talking about myself."

"Well tell me," Rachel said, "what is it you do for a living?"

"Well," Frankie said, repeating what he normally told the chicks he went on dates with, "my friend Miles and I started up a business a little over a year ago."

"Oh, that sounds exciting," Rachel said, her curiosity clearly piqued.

"Yeah, I guess it is," he said.

"What does your business do?" She asked.

"Well it's a small, little video and photography business," Frankie said with a smirk.

"Like weddings and stuff?" Rachel asked.

"Yeah," Frankie said as he took a sip of his bourbon on the rocks. "Something like that."

Frankie thought about going on, but before he could he felt a tap of his shoulder. He looked over to see a douche-bag standing very close to his table. The douche was wearing a backwards, flat-billed baseball cap, a tank top, and shorts (which was not how one should dress in the certain establishment they were in).

"Hey man," the douche-bag said as he leaned in closer

to Frankie. "Sorry to bother you, but aren't you Frankie Wood?"

Frankie couldn't think of anything to say off the top of his head. All he did was just look at Rachel as though the douche-bag was a crazy person and shakes his head.

"No," the douche-bag said as he leaned in even closer to Frankie and eyed him. "It is you!" The douche, letting his drunkenness show more and more, then turned away from Frankie and shouted off, "It's him!"

Frankie, whose heart was beating erratically at that moment, looked over to where the douche-bag called off and saw that there were two more assholes sitting at a table across the restaurant.

"Frankie!" One of the assholes called out. "You fucking rock, man!"

"Your chicks are *the* hottest, dude!" The other asshole yelled across the rather-nice restaurant.

"What the hell is going on, Frank?" Rachel asked, looking at the assholes, then the douche-bag, and finally, Frankie.

"Oh shit," the douche chimed in, before Frankie could make up an excuse. "Is this chick your new girlfriend, Frankie?"

"*New* girlfriend?" Rachel asked, clearly offended.

"I-" Frankie tried to begin, but then the douche-bag interrupted again.

"Dude," the douche said, completely ignoring the awkward tension he had forced upon two strangers, "that one chick you had- the fucking Asian one with the dyed hair or whatever -she's fucking hot! I mean hot, dude!

Like with two t's. Hott, you know? You gotta get more of her, bro."

"Look, man," said Frankie, realizing that the awkwardness needed to be stopped at that point. "I'm just trying to eat, alright?" He stood up to face the douche-bag.

"Oh shit, sorry man," the douche-bag said, seeming to finally realize where he was, "I'm just so pumped to meet you. *Frankie's' Girlfriends* is like my absolute favorite site out there. It's definitely my favorite. I mean, I know it's only been around for a minute and you've only got like ten or fifteen girls up there, but it still fucking rocks."

"Well thanks, really," Frankie said, letting the flattery get the best of him, "I appreciate it. But listen man, I really have to get back to my dinner."

"Yeah, man, of course," the douche-bag seemed to be a little bit more well-behaved than he had previously let on, "I'm sorry. But hey, do you think I could maybe get an autograph? I'm really sorry if I bugged you."

"You did, but it's fine," Frankie said with a smile. "Of course I'll sign something for you."

Frankie then reached into his pocket and pulled out a pin and a business card. He signed *Frankie Wood* and handed the card to the douche-bag. The douche-bag took it as though it were some sort of sacred document and held it in both his hands.

"Thanks, man," the douche said.

"No problem," Frankie said as he patted him on the shoulder.

The douche-bag then walked off, heading back to his

table, holding the card up, over his head, valiantly.

Frankie looked at Rachel with a strange "I don't know what to say" look as he retook his seat.

"Look, I…" Frankie began to say, even though he had no idea what the fuck he was going to say.

"Are you a pornographer?" Rachel asked him point blank.

"Yes," Frankie said, knowing that all of the work he'd put in with her was fucked beyond belief.

"And were you going to try to photograph me? Or us?" Rachel asked.

"Yes," said Frankie. What did he have to lose?

Rachel then looked away from Frankie with a little scoff as though she couldn't believe what she was hearing. She looked around the restaurant and bit her lip as she thought about everything that had just happened. Then, to Frankie's surprise, she turned to Frankie and smirked.

"How much does it pay?" She then asked.

Frankie smirked back at her and ran his fingers over his mouth and down his chin.

"I'm sure we can come up with something," he said.

And before he knew it, Rachel was back at Miles' place on his couch, laying on her back, her knees bent, her feet up. Frankie rammed his cock into her at a rapid pace as she moaned and moaned and moaned.

"Cum on my fucking tits," she said as she gasped between moans.

"Okay," Frankie said, breathing heavy.

"No," Rachel said. "Fucking cum on my face."

"Okay," Frankie said with a smirk. "Get on your knees.

Frankie pulled out of her and she hopped off the couch. She got down on her knees and tilted her head up, just under Frankie's cock with her mouth open and her tongue out. Frankie then came all over her. A spurt slashed across her face, another caught on her tongue. More cum came and it fell upon her chin and dripped down to her tits. The last eruption shot out, over her face and into her hair. She was smiling all the while.

The video that Frankie recorded that night went on to be the most viewed video on the site at that time.

---

Months later, Frankie and Rachel sat on Miles' couch as Miles was busy working on the computer. Frankie sat there with tinfoil wrapped around his head. Various hair-bleaching products were strewn across the coffee table. Frankie couldn't help but keep scratching his head; it itched something fierce.

"Don't scratch it!" Rachel said, eyeing Frankie like a fox. "You'll fuck it up."

"It burns," Frankie said. "Is that normal?"

"It's supposed to burn a little," Rachel said. "Leave it alone."

"Ugh," Frankie said.

He then stood up and walked to the kitchen and grabbed a beer from the fridge. Without asking if they wanted one, he grabbed one for Rachel and Miles. He walked back into the living room and handed one to Miles and then one to Rachel.

They both said thank you.

"You sure you've done this before?" Frankie asked Rachel as he cracked his beer open.

"No," Rachel said as she opened her beer. "But I've seen it done a million times."

"What?" Frankie asked, almost spitting his beer out. "God damn it, Rachel."

"Don't blame me," Rachel said, taking a swig. "You wanted it done cheap."

Frankie just shook his head.

"I don't know why you even want this done," Miles said, spinning around his chair and popping his beer can open. "Only douchers have bleached hair."

"I can't keep getting recognized, man," Frankie said, sipping his beer. "It happened *again*. Not every chick is as cool as Rachel."

"True dat," Rachel said as she lifted her can in a cheers-like fashion. "Speaking of being cool, do you guys fuck around with blow?"

"Blow?" Frankie asked. "Like cocaine?"

"Yeah, like '*cocaine*,'" Rachel said with a mocking laugh. "You guys ever done it before?"

"Nope," said Frankie.

"One time," Miles said, "I guess I liked it well enough. Made me a little erratic."

"Do you guys want to do some?" Rachel then asked, going to her purse and digging around.

"I think I'll take a pass on that," Miles said, "I've still got some work to do."

"What's it like?" Frankie asked.

"You know that energized feeling you get right after

you cum?" Rachel asked, pulling out a little baggie of white powder.

"Yeah," Frankie said. "Is it like that?"

"Better," Rachel said as she pulled out a compact that had been washed clean of make-up.

"Well damn," Frankie said. "If that's true I think I've got to give it a shot. Do we do it on that thing?" Frankie motioned to the compact.

"Usually," Rachel said. "But if you want, you can do it off my tits. I've always wanted to do that."

"Fucking sold," Frankie said. "Take off that shirt and let's do this."

"Are you going to film it?" Miles asked.

"I don't know if we can use it, can we? I mean…" Frankie said smirking and thinking. "I guess I can keep it for my personal files. Get the camera, Miles."

"You have personal files?" Rachel asked as Miles walked out of the room.

"Yeah, some," Frankie said, "I mean, they're just kind of like bloopers."

"Alright," said Miles as he walked back into the room with the camera in his hand, "Where should I shoot from?"

Frankie thought about it as Rachel took off her shirt. She then began to sprinkle the cocaine onto her left breast from the baggie.

"Don't you have to like cut that with a card or something?" Frankie asked. "Isn't that what they do in movies?"

"You don't have to do that with good shit," Rachel

said. "Now come on before it sticks to my skin." She then handed him a pen that had been hollowed out and cut in half.

"Alright," Frankie said as he took the pen. "Miles, get it from like over my shoulder."

Miles positioned himself behind Frankie and lined up the shot in a way that he thought was aesthetically pleasing.

"That's the spot," Frankie said to Miles, he then turned to Rachel. "Alright, lets do this."

He then put the pen in his nose and leaned down to the tip of the line that Rachel had made just above her nipple. He snorted in deep (like he'd seen it done in the movies) and he could feel it burn as the powder went straight up his nose. He then felt a numbness in his nasal cavity and it started to drip down the back of his throat.

"Ah!" Frankie said, feeling kind of powerful in that moment, "I did cocaine!" He said proudly, he then turned to the camera, "I fucking did cocaine."

"You sure did, baby," Rachel said, smiling at Frankie's excitement. "What do you think?"

"I think I'm in love," Frankie said, inhaling sharply through his nose. "Are there more things like this? There's got to be. What about heroin?"

"Heroin's alright," Rachel said, "I've only ever snorted it; I'm afraid of needles."

"Could you get some?" Frankie asked, excitement in his eyes.

"What?" Rachel asked with a laugh. "Like right now?"

"Yeah," Frankie said. "Why not? I want to do all the drugs. Fuck it."

"How about we just stick to coke tonight," Rachel said. "We should wait until your hair is dry before we delve any deeper."

"Alright," Frankie said. "Pour me another line." He then turned to Miles. "We need more angles, yeah?"

"If you say so," Miles said as he moved to a different place.

Rachel made another line on her tit with a deftness that showed that she had done it before.

Frankie put the pen back up his nose and snorted the blow up it. Nothing had really ever felt that good. And nothing would ever feel that good again.

---

Frankie caught a glimpse of himself in a reflection on the large-screened TV he had just bought. Even though it wasn't a proper, mirror-like reflection, he could still size himself up appropriately. He looked very relaxed, but he could tell that his blonde hair was growing out. He wondered if it had really been that long as he continued to sit up against the base of the couch on the floor.

He thought about asking Rachel to touch up his hair, but he didn't want to bother her at the moment, she seemed very drunk and he thought he might be too high to speak anyway.

Heroin had proved to be a wonderful drug. Its high was akin to the one someone would get from laying in the grass, while the last little bit of summer sun washed over them as a cool fall breeze swept in. Except ten-fold. No, a thousand-fold. It was positively amazing.

He'd done other stuff, different drugs, since he'd dove into cocaine, but (if he wasn't doing coke) heroin was one of his most frequently used substances. It was like a security blanket or doing yoga after a hard week. It set him positively right and he felt oh-so happy.

His hand moved from his side and it took him a moment to realize that Rachel had reached down from the couch to hold it.

"You doing okay?" She asked in a drunken slur.

"Yeah," Frankie said, "I feel real great. I just don't want to move around. I'm afraid I'll puke again."

"Yeah, you can't move on H," Rachel said. "At least not too much. It makes you puke. Like every time. I wonder why that is."

"I dunno," Frankie said, "I flunked biology in high school."

A nice silence then fell over the room. He liked that he could have these silences with her. Sure, they were drug induced (usually), but that didn't make them any less pleasant. They'd known each other for a year now and it seemed like their friendship had expanded into something that Frankie really enjoyed. Unfortunately, Frankie felt as though he didn't let Rachel know it enough.

"Hey, Rachel," Frankie said as he squeezed her hand slightly with his.

"Yes, Frankie," Rachel replied, giving him a little squeeze back.

"You know, I'm in love with you, right?" Frankie asked, trying to turn his head to face her, but not wanting to induce vomiting.

"You don't love me," Rachel said with a laugh. "You're just feeling lonely."

"I know…" Frankie said, suddenly feeling bad for bringing love up at all. "Why do you think I'm so lonely all the time?"

"Because you like it that way," Rachel said, letting go of Frankie's hand and rolling over, away from him. "I'm tired."

Frankie wanted to talk more about his loneliness, but he was also enjoying basking in the warmth that was radiating through his body. He got lost thinking about it for a second and shut his eyes for a moment. For some reason, in that moment, Maxine's face conjured itself up in his mind. That moment wasn't a moment, though. It lasted for a while.

Frankie didn't know how it happened, but when he opened his eyes the sun was setting out the window. Frankie could have thought that it was noon, but the sun begged to differ. He wondered where Rachel was.

"Hey?" Frankie asked.

"Yes?" Rachel responded, seemingly half asleep, still lying on the couch behind him.

"Will you marry me?" Frankie asked in the direction he thought that Rachel was. He could feel her moving on the couch.

"No, Frankie," Rachel said with a laugh. "You've got to stop asking me." There was playful agitation in her tone.

"Okay, Maxine," Frankie said. "That's fair enough."

"What?" Rachel asked, acting like she misheard the wrong name, but clearly knowing what he said.

"I-" Frankie said, before he was cut off by the unwitting Miles as he entered the room.

"Hey Frankie," Miles said as he walked in.

"Yeah?" Frankie asked, glad that Miles had walked in at that moment.

"We're up to a million subscribers," Miles said with an excitement Frankie had rarely heard.

"Does that mean we're rich?" Frankie asked with a laugh.

"Yeah," Miles said. "We're fucking rich, dude."

"Well goddamn," Frankie said as he stood up and immediately regretted it. He must've still been feeling the heroin despite how much time had passed, so he sat back down again. "We should buy a house. Like a porn house. Maybe we can start shooting proper shit. We can use Rachel or maybe that Denise girl."

"*Denise*-Denise?" Miles asked with a laugh. "Didn't we fuck her over?"

"I think we fuck everyone over," Frankie said.

"Yeah, that's true," Miles said, having to agree with the sad truth. "But I think Denise is especially a no-go."

"Well what about, Rachel?" Frankie asked before he turned around and looked at her. "What do you think? Should I buy a house and shoot porn there?"

"I don't see why not," Rachel said with a shrug, "I'd be in them if the pay was good."

"Don't we pay you well?" Frankie asked, a little offended.

"You still owe me a check," Rachel said, hiding her seriousness behind a smile.

"I'd write you one now," Frankie said before he brought his hands up and squeezed them in and out of fists. "But my fingers feel funny."

Just then, before negotiations could commence, there was a knock on the door. Hearing that made Frankie look at Miles. A panic shot through them as they looked at one another. No one ever knocked on their door. Well that wasn't completely true; it was just that the people who knocked on their door usually wanted to start shit. That is to say, no one *good* ever knocked on their door.

"I'll get it," Miles said, swallowing the anxiety down and walking over to the door.

Frankie decided to close his eyes again. The brown high wasn't quite done, but it had definitely peaked. He wasn't feeling as good as he needed to. He thought about doing more.

Before he could, he heard Miles open the door and a commotion ensued.

"Holy fuck," Miles said before he called back into the room. "Frankie, you better run!"

Frankie didn't have the time to open his eyes before he heard footsteps approach him and felt a foot make contact with his gut.

"Mother-fucker!" Frankie yelled out in pain. He closed his eyes tighter as he gripped his stomach in pain.

"No, you're the mother-fucker, you piece-of-shit," said a voice that Frankie had not heard in quite some time. It was obviously the voice of Maxine.

Frankie's eyes shot open and he looked up at her in disbelief.

"What the fuck is going on?" he asked, not knowing if he could trust his eyes.

"Fuck you, Francis," Maxine said; her anger was making her shake.

"What the fuck, Maxine?" Frankie asked.

"You're such a piece-of-shit!" Maxine shouted.

"Yeah, I know," Frankie said.

"Oh my god," Maxine laughed, but she was not amused, "I cannot believe you, Francis. Or is it *Frankie* now?"

"What?" Frankie asked, clearly very confused, and still in pain from the kick to his gut.

"*Frankiesgirlfriends.com*?" Maxine said as though she might kick him again. "Really, Francis?"

"Oh god damn it," Frankie said, finally realizing what was, in fact, going on. "Miles! Get the checkbook!"

"Checkbook?" Maxine asked. "What? You think I want a fucking payoff?"

"You don't?" Frankie said as he moved to his feet. His head began to spin; he had gotten up too fast again.

"No," Maxine said matter-of-factly, "I don't. I want a cut and I want in."

"What?" Frankie asked. "Why?" His head would not stop spinning.

"I've seen your numbers," Maxine said. "I've also seen the comments. I know I made you. I think it's what I deserve, you fucking asshole."

"Oh…" Frankie said as the room kept moving around and around and around.

"Are you alright?" Rachel could be heard asking as

Frankie moved his hands about, trying to grab on to something that would make the world stand still.

"I think I did too much heroin," Frankie said as he felt his knees slowly begin to buckle.

"Are you doing heroin now?" Maxine asked, more concerned than angry.

"Are you really here?" He asked just before his legs finally gave way and he fell to the floor, facing the ceiling.

Frankie then saw Maxine walk over to him and stand over him. Tunnel vision began to set in and his world began to get blacker and blacker around the edges.

"Francis?" Maxine asked, looking down at him.

The world then went completely black, his mind was leaving rapidly, but before it went away completely, he could still hear her voice calling.

"Francis?" She asked from the darkness. "Francis…"

# THE 5<sup>TH</sup> ACT OF
# THE GREATEST PORNO EVER MADE

His name was Frankie Wood and he was lying on the floor of his disgusting bathroom. It was in the house he'd bought when he used to love making pornography. It wasn't always his house, but it was his house now.

There was a pounding coming from the door and it woke him up. He looked around to see that he was surrounded by baggies of drugs and other shit. The pounding started giving him a headache as soon as he opened his eyes.

"Frankie?" Called Maxine's voice through the door. "We know you're in there."

Frankie stood up and held his head. He was still high, but not the right kind. He thought about trying to figure out what he could do to remedy that, but the pounding on the door needed to be taken care of first.

He opened the door with a huff and saw Maxine and Miles standing there. Maxine looked pissed, Miles looked worried. They seemed to perpetually be that way now, whenever Frankie saw them

"Oh Jesus," Maxine said when she saw Frankie; she turned to Miles. "How long was he fucking in there?"

"I don't know," Miles said, "I lost track of time. I was trying to calm everybody down."

"Frankie," she said when she turned back to him. "Are you high?"

"The fuck you think, Maxine?" Frankie said as he rubbed his eyes.

"I think you and I need to have a conversation," Maxine said.

"Alright," Frankie said. "Just give me a second."

"No," Maxine said. "Now."

"Well alright then," Frankie said, forcing the fakest smile he could muster onto his face. "What's shakin' bacon?"

"Not here," Maxine said. "It smells like shit."

"Alright," Frankie said. "Where then?"

"Outside?" Maxine asked, but it was more of a command than a question.

"Ugh," Frankie said, as though it would put him out beyond all belief. "Fine. But Miles is coming too, he's as much a part of this company as either of us."

"Nah, dude, I'm-" Miles tried to say.

"Fine," Maxine said, before Miles could finish, "I'd like to talk to both of you anyway."

Miles rolled his eyes but conceded nonverbally.

Frankie then motioned for Maxine to lead the way and then followed her as she walked through the house and to the back porch. He lit up a smoke as soon as he was outside.

"Okay," Maxine said, not wanting to waste any time. "First things first: What did I tell you about shooting up in the bathroom?"

"Several more first things first:" Frankie began as he started to count his short list off on his fingers, "I didn't shoot up, I snorted it; it's *my* fucking bathroom; and when did you turn into the dictator of this place? We all paid for this place."

"Yeah," Maxine said. "But you paid me for it. This is my childhood home, Frankie. I had rules for a reason. You agreed to them when I let you buy it. I don't want you shitting on my childhood."

"Fine," Frankie said, "I'm not going to make promises, but I'll try to be more respectful."

"I'm not-" Maxine began, before she realized it might not be worth it. "No, you know what, we'll put a pin in that. What we really have to talk about is how you can't fire Rachel and James."

"Are you serious?" Frankie said, not wanting to fight with Maxine for the umpteenth time. "Rachel I get, but James? All James does is give me shitty fucking clichés."

Maxine just looked at Frankie and scoffed, almost disgusted.

"What?" Frankie asked.

"Nothing," Maxine said, her tone rife with sarcasm, "I just wasn't aware that a guy who came up with another *ex-girlfriend* site could ride such a fucking high horse."

"That's exactly what I'm talking about, Maxine!"

Frankie said incredulously, "I don't want to keep making the same shit. I don't want the shit we're doing now to turn into the 'ex-girlfriend' thing. I don't want our next idea to go bust."

Maxine sighed. It was clear that she was reaching her breaking point.

"I'm not being crazy," Frankie said, "I know I'm crazy, but I'm not being crazy about this."

"Just make the fucking movie, Frankie," Maxine said as she rubbed her eyes and took the cigarette from Frankie's mouth. She took a long drag. "Please."

"No," Frankie said, taking the cigarette back when Maxine was done, "I'm so fucking done with clichés."

"God damn it, Frankie," she said as she, again, took the cigarette from Frankie. "Why do you have to make things so difficult?"

"I'm not trying to be difficult, Maxine," Frankie said, deciding it might be better to just leave the cigarette to Maxine and light up another.

"What's it going to take to get you to do this shit?" Maxine asked, clearly at the end of her rope. It was a tone Frankie knew quite well.

"Do the fucking gangbang," Frankie said, as he said countless times before when trying to bargain with Maxine. He knew he sounded like a broken record, but the popular opinion from the fans of Frankie Wood, was that Maxine needed to get back into the movies they were shooting. He knew if she did come back, it would have to be big. "If you agree to do the gangbang I'll march right back in there and finish James off myself."

"No," Maxine said, "I've already told you I'm not going to do it."

"C'mon," Frankie pleaded.

"I've said no a thousand times," Maxine said. "How many more times do you want me to say it?"

"You're still our highest rated actress," Frankie argued. "Everyone wants to see you again."

"I retired," Maxine said flatly.

"So, come out of it," Frankie said with a shrug.

"How are gangbangs not cliché?" Maxine asked.

"Gangbangs with beautiful girls aren't cliché," Frankie explained. "They're like a fucking golden egg, man."

"So why can't Rachel do it?" Maxine asked, stomping out the cigarette.

"Rachel's too porn-star-y," Frankie said point blank, it was clear he'd entertained that notion before.

"Well, I'm not going to do it, Frankie," Maxine said, just as point blank as Frankie's previous statement.

"Then I'm not going to make a movie that's going to fucking bomb," Frankie said.

"It won't bomb," Maxine retorted as she rolled her eyes.

"Yes, it fucking will," Frankie said before he turned to Miles. "Will you tell her it's going to fucking bomb?"

"Oh, no," Miles said, clearly a little perturbed to have to watch another Frankie/Maxine fight. "I'm going to stay out of this."

"Ugh," Maxine said, clearly tired of dealing with Frankie. "Look, Frankie, if it bombs…" Maxine couldn't even finish her thought, though.

"Yes?" Frankie asked, trying to pry it out of her. He'd known Maxine for quite some time (in several different capacities) and he could tell what the look on her face was suggesting. It made him excited.

"I'll do the gangbang," Maxine said with a sigh, but then she knew she needed to add restrictions. "But I absolutely will not do D.V.D.A. Or D.V. or D.A. No double-dicking of any kind."

"God damn it, fine," Frankie said, clearly pissed with the caveats. "But you've also got to give me carte blanche on one other project, okay?"

"Oh, for fuck's sake, if I give you a fucking inch…" she said, she then shook her head, as though she knew better. She then agreed, somewhat reluctantly. "Yes, okay? Now go make the movie."

"All hail Maxine! Maxine: The Boner Queen!" Frankie said as he goose-stepped around the back porch saluting like a Nazi.

Maxine and Miles shook their heads as they watched Frankie celebrate in his weird, stupid way he was wont to do.

"Let's go make a shitty movie!" Frankie then said in a German accent as he clapped his hands and marched inside.

Maxine looked at Miles. Miles just shrugged and followed after him. Maxine sighed and shook her head.

When Frankie walked into the garage, he saw that the crew was dismantling the set. Tony, the Director of Photography, seemed to have taken charge. He was bossing people around here and there.

"Yeah, keep the door the way it is," Tony said, to a man who was standing by the stage door, before he turned to another man near a bookshelf. "Keep the shelves up, but put all the shit on them in a box, okay? Try to make it look neat."

Frankie walked up to Tony, but Tony hadn't noticed that Frankie had re-entered the room. No one had, for that matter.

"What the fuck is going on?" Frankie snapped, which made Tony jump.

"Oh shit, Frankie," Tony said when he saw Frankie. He then tried to explain, "You told us to-"

"Fuck you, Tony," Frankie said, putting his hand up as though he was done letting Tony speak. "Set it up again."

Tony glanced over to Miles as Miles entered the room. They shared a concerned glance they'd shared many times as Frankie looked around.

"Where the fuck are James and Rachel?" Frankie asked everyone before he spotted them standing near the garage door, comforting each other. "James! Rachel!"

Rachel saw Frankie coming before James did and she rolled her eyes. James saw her rolling her eyes and looked over to see what it was that caused her to do that. Once he saw him, James also rolled his eyes and approached Frankie before he could get too close to Rachel.

"What do you want, Frankie?" James asked, sternly.

"Look, man," Frankie said putting his hands up to show he wasn't looking for a fight. "I just wanted to tell you that I'm sorry."

"Fuck you," James said with scorn. "That shit ain't

going to work this time around."

"James, man, seriously," Frankie said, trying to sound as calm as possible. "You know me. I just- I just lose it sometimes. And you know I like you James. I mean shit; I wanted you for the movies from the moment we met. You remember that don't you?"

When Frankie said that, he hoped that James' mind would go back in time to the first time they met. Back then, Frankie was freshly blonde (not from the first dye-job he'd had done, but maybe the third or fourth). He had walked into a convenience store and saw James standing there.

James had been eyeing the candy near the register, trying to decide which one sounded the best at that particular moment.

Frankie had walked passed him and looked him up and down. James didn't see him do it, however (Frankie was discrete). Frankie then walked to the counter and the cashier nodded to him.

"Can I get a pack of Gilded Spirits," Frankie said as he pointed to the cigarettes behind the cashier. "The yellow ones please."

"Yellow?" The cashier had asked, as though he hadn't heard, even though he clearly had.

"Yes," Frankie said, with an eye roll, he knew he'd been heard.

He then watched as the cashier grabbed the pack of cigarettes and rang them up. Frankie then put a ten-dollar bill on the counter and grabbed the pack of smokes, beginning to pocket them as soon as he'd lifted them.

"Keep the change," Frankie had told the cashier.

Frankie then went to walk away and had turned to the door before the nagging feeling hit him. He turned and looked back at James.

"Excuse me," Frankie had said, it was the first words he'd ever said to James, "I don't mean to be overly rude, but if you had to estimate, how big do you think your cock is?"

James had just stared at Frankie as they both stood there in the middle of the convenience store for what felt like a really long time. He then answered Frankie honestly and the rest, as they say, became history.

Frankie smiled as that memory washed over him, and he hoped that James remembered it too, now that they were standing in the garage.

"Yes, of course I remember," James said, clearly trying to hide a smile.

"Then you know how important you are to this team, James," Frankie said, grabbing James by the shoulders. "So please let's finish this."

"Okay," James said after he had looked at Frankie for a while and contemplated what Frankie had said. "But Frankie, man, you've got to stop treating me like shit."

"Deal," Frankie said, too quickly to actually mean it, he then walked to Rachel. "And you. You! Think about all we've been through together, Rachel. I mean you've been here since the beginning."

Frankie couldn't help but remember a time when Rachel's legs were wrapped around him and they clutched him dearly and passionately.

"You know I can't stay mad at you," Rachel said, sincerely. It would seem more sincere if she hadn't decided to start speaking in her stupid, southern accent again.

"Good, I'm glad," Frankie said with a niceness he wasn't known for. He then went back to being an asshole at the drop of a hat. "But seriously, drop the accent when we aren't shooting. It's fucking annoying."

"You know I have to stay in character, Frankie," said Rachel, not dropping the accent.

"That's bullshit. You aren't fucking Tom Pell," Frankie said, turning away from her. "And this is fucking porn."

Frankie noticed that everyone was looking at him as he spoke to the actors and no one seemed to do anything. He clapped his hands loudly and shouted so that they could snap out of whatever trance they were in.

"Alright, people, let's do this!" Frankie shouted as he walked over to his director's chair, just as Miles came up and handed him a script.

"We're all good to go, chief," Miles said.

"Perfect," Frankie said, he then addressed the crew. "Let's roll tape."

"What about-" Tony started to ask.

"Just roll the tape, Tony." Frankie barked.

Tony quickly moved to the camera and pressed the record button.

"Rolling!" he yelled out.

"Good," Frankie said. "Actors! Places!"

Frankie watched and waited as the actor positioned themselves.

"Let's go ahead and start with penetration, I think we've got enough expositional, shit," Frankie said.

He then waited as they positioned themselves. Something wasn't right about their placement though. It took Frankie a while to realize what it was.

"Can we play with your ass, Rachel?" Frankie asked.

"Sure," said Rachel. "No anal though. Just fingers please."

"Cool, thanks, can do," said Frankie. "James, go ahead and move up to her ass."

James clearly knew very little about human anatomy.

"No, James, no!" Frankie yelled. "Her asshole! Get at her goddamn asshole."

James then put his thumb on her asshole as Rachel cheated it towards the camera.

"Perfect, thank you," Frankie said before he turned to Miles. "We good?"

"Yep," Miles said. "Looks good."

"Alright, penetration on 'action!' Let's make some magic people," Frankie then positioned himself appropriately, he wasn't going to close his eyes this time. "Action!"

James shoved his big black cock into Rachel's wet-on-demand pussy and she let out a long-exaggerated moan that sounded not fake, but definitely over exaggerated.

Frankie sighed loudly into his hand.

---

When Frankie had negotiated the sale of Maxine's parents' house to his company, he had lamented the fact that it didn't have a conference room. He had wanted to make the business more legitimate and so he had been fairly adamant that they have a place where they could hold meetings. Miles and Maxine had discussed it (as Frankie's business partners) with Frankie and decided that they could turn Maxine's parent's dining room into a conference room.

That's where they found themselves now, sitting around the table they'd bought, Maxine and Miles staring as Frankie as he stared right back on them, a huge, dumbass smile on his face. He was too excited to speak. He could barely contain his excitement.

"What are you waiting for, Frankie?" Maxine said. "Just fucking say it."

"Yeah," Miles added. "Just get it over with."

Frankie didn't want to just get it over with, though; he wanted to relish this moment. It was worthy of savoring. He so enjoyed being right.

"Frankie, just-" Maxine, nearly at her wits end, tried to speak, but Frankie couldn't hold it in any longer.

"I fucking told you so, bi-otch!" Frankie yelled, as obnoxiously as he could. He then laughed and laughed for what had to be a very long time.

Soon, his hysteria died down and he caught his breath.

"Satisfied?" Maxine asked, not amused by Frankie's antics.

"Yes, very," Frankie said with a smug look on his face, "I mean, ha! I knew the movie was going to be a shit-show, but our lowest grossing project to date? Who could have known? Oh yeah... me!"

Frankie then let out a burst of laughter again and picked up a legal pad with some points-of-order he'd written down. He motioned for Maxine and Miles to go to their legal pads. Miles did, Maxine didn't. She never did. She just kept her arms folded and rolled her eyes at Frankie.

"Alright," Frankie said, trying to act professional, "I hereby call this meeting to order. The first thing on our agenda is that I want to start shooting A.S.A.P. How long will it take to get actors?"

"A week, maybe two," Miles said as he wrote something down on his legal pad, "I don't really know; I'll put out an open call."

"Wait, wait, wait," Maxine interjected. "How many cocks are we talking about?"

"Fifteen or twenty," Frankie said, trying to ballpark it, "I want it to be a relatively large group, though. Maybe we can do something larger. Will you write that down, Miles?"

Miles wrote *fifteen-twenty (or larger)* on his legal pad.

"No way!" Maxine said. "That is way too many. Two or three tops."

"Maxine, this has to be huge!" Frankie argued.

"No way," Maxine said, standing her ground. "Absolutely not."

"You agreed!" Frankie said, it could plainly be seen that he was about to throw a temper tantrum.

"Fuck you," Maxine said, not wanting to argue.

"Oh yeah, speaking of fucking me," Frankie said, dropping the temper tantrum route in exchange for just ignoring Maxine's objections. "I was thinking about doing a director cameo."

"Look, Frankie," Maxine said, "I'm not going to do this if it's more than three, okay?"

"Alright," Frankie said. "Can I propose a compromise?"

"I'd rather you didn't," Maxine said, growing tired of Frankie's nonsense.

"Oh c'mon," Frankie said. "You always fucking do this, Maxine. You always renege. We had a fucking deal; you said you would do this. You can't say you won't. I'm open to a discussion about it, but you're going to have to meet me halfway. You can't be that kid who takes their ball home when they're losing"

"Well give me fucking options then," Maxine said, "I don't want to have to jack-off guys with a dick in my butt, pussy, and mouth. Nothing about that seems fun in the slightest."

"Okay," Frankie said. "See I can work with this. Let's see… What if we did like a train thing, then? Like groups. Three guys at a time."

"Two guys at a time," Maxine said. "I don't want to have to commit to anal every time, okay?"

"You've got to do anal, Maxine," Frankie said.

"I know I have to," Maxine spat. "This isn't my first rodeo. All I'm saying is I don't want to have to do it *a lot*."

"Um, sure," Frankie said, thinking. "We can do something about that, I think. What if we did the train thing, three guys, like I said, but one guy's a masturbator who you can direct on the fly?"

"Like he just jerks-off?" Maxine asked, thinking about the idea.

"Well yeah, but sometimes you tell him to fuck your ass or you give him a hand or put him in your mouth," Frankie said. "He's like a jack of all trades, you know?"

"Okay," Maxine said, "I like that. So it'll just be two guys in me at a given time with the option of the third?"

"Yep, but you are going to have to do anal sometimes. Sound good, Miles?" Frankie turned to Miles to get his opinion.

"Yeah, I think that could work," Miles said. "How many guys in total though?"

"What about fifty?" Frankie said.

"You said twenty before," Maxine said.

"Yeah, but I thought about it," Frankie said. "It's got to be something special. In this business, special equals bigger. We've got to go big. It's not like I'm saying a hundred. Now that would be absurd."

"What about thirty?" Maxine said. "That's already ten groups. That will seem like a lot."

"Thirty-one," Frankie said, "I want to go solo. We can bill it as our big reunion."

"Alright, fine," Maxine said. "Let's talk cum."

"What about it?" Frankie said.

"Where's it going to happen?" Maxine asked. "I'd rather it all not go on my face."

"We could," Miles chimed in, "do like 'drench her' kind of thing. You know? Where we just cover her in cum."

"Like we assign each guy an area and he fills that up?" Frankie asked.

"I like that idea," Maxine said, "I mean it'll be messy, but as long as it doesn't all wind up in my hair and mouth I think I'll be okay."

"I call twat!" Frankie said. "Write it down Miles."

Miles wrote down *Frankie calls twat* on his legal pad.

"No one's coming inside of me, Frankie, not even you," said Maxine, putting her foot down before he got the ball rolling.

"I don't want to cum *inside you*, Maxine," Frankie said with a mocking giggle. "Jeez, someone is vain."

"Alright, fine," Maxine said. "Sounds good. Miles, I'll need some valium for this, okay? And make sure we've got enough lube this time. I don't want a repeat of 'The Rachel Situation.' She couldn't work for a week."

Miles wrote *Get Valium & Lube* down.

"Is that it?" Frankie asked.

"I think so, for now," Maxine said, "I might have some more concerns as I think about it, but I think this is a good jumping off point."

"I think it sounds good," Miles said.

"Good," Frankie said. "Then that is that; meeting adjourned."

They all then got up and walked out of the room. Frankie lit up a smoke and smiled to Maxine. She smirked back to him, but there was something vacant in her eyes. Frankie thought about it for a moment as she walked off, heading upstairs. He then turned to Miles once she was gone.

"You really think this is a good idea?" Frankie asked, letting his rarely seen insecurity show.

"Oh yeah," Miles said, "this might be the best idea you've ever had.

---

Two weeks passed by pretty quickly and soon Frankie found himself standing on line behind nine robed men. He wore a robe himself. They were queued behind a red curtain that separated them from, what Frankie called, The Gangbang Arena. Rachel stood at the front of the line with a clipboard, peeking out every so often to see when she needed to send the next group out.

"How's it looking?" Frankie asked her several times throughout the shoot.

"Looks good," Rachel had replied every time he asked.

Frankie was nervous. From what he could hear it sounded like it was going *well*, but it needed to be better than well. It needed to be *great*. It was Maxine's comeback, for fuck's sake; mediocrity just wouldn't do.

He'd spared no expense. He'd bought more cameras and a new bed (complete with fancy red sheets). He'd also bought large red curtains to match the sheets. He'd hired men to hang them around the garage and more to man the cameras he demanded circle the bed. He set the camera angles and color and contrast himself. Perfection needed to be achieved.

Honestly, he felt that this film could be the perfection he had been seeking.

"Hey man," Miles said as he walked up. He too was robed, but unlike the ones still in line, he was sweaty, a film of moisture made his hair cling to his head. The look of him took Frankie's mind off his incessant need to fret over perfection.

"How was it?" Frankie asked.

"Great, man," Miles said, "I think it's going good."

"That's good," Frankie said. "Did you cum on your space?"

"Kinda," Miles said, "I *aimed* for her throat, but I hit her chin and hair. I think some got on her tits too. I don't know man; I was into it. It's hard to aim."

"That's fine I guess," Frankie said, "I mean close enough, right?"

"Yeah," Miles answered. "That's how I'm looking at it. Shit though, I am tired."

"Yeah it seems like this is taking longer than I thought it would," Frankie said.

"Well it's Maxine we're talking about here, man," Miles said. "I think that everyone wants to take their time with it, you know? Like enjoy it. This is a once-in-a-lifetime kind of thing."

"Not for me," Frankie said. "Do you think she looks tired?"

"Yeah, I guess," Miles said. "But I am beat. I need to go lie down. Come and get me when it's done."

"Cool, will do," Frankie said as Miles gave a little, playful salute and walked off.

Frankie could feel his nerves getting the better of him. He hadn't done any of the normal drugs he was used to doing throughout the day (at least not in the quantities he was accustomed to). Sure, he'd done a few bumps of coke and he *had to* drink, but other than that, he'd stayed relatively sober. He wanted to keep his head clear for the task at hand.

The task at hand, however, was proving to be too much for him to handle. It could be the sobriety, but he was shaking a little. It was more of a shiver, but it seemed to affect him down to his bones.

"Alright!" Rachel's voice broke into Frankie's mind as she called to the line of men. "The next group can enter now."

Frankie then watched as Rachel waved the next three guys into The Gangbang Arena.

"Make it quick, boys," she said as they passed her, before she closed the curtain behind them.

That caused Frankie's ears to perk up and he waved to Rachel. Once he got her attention he motioned for her to come to his side.

"What's up, Frankie?" Rachel asked as she walked up to him.

"How's it looking?" Frankie asked.

"It looks fine, Frankie," Rachel said, a little perturbed at how often she'd had to answer the question. "It's going to be good, quit stressing."

"Well," Frankie said, "I'm just a little *concerned* about her, you know? Miles said she looked tired. I'm worried this is taking too long."

"She's definitely getting tuckered out," Rachel said. "I mean one gangbang scene can take a lot out of you, but ten? That's quite the workload."

"Fuck," Frankie said. "This might have been a bad idea."

"Well it's a little late now," Rachel said with a laugh. "I mean, what do you want to do?"

"Cut the rest," Frankie said, without thinking.

"What?" Rachel asked with a laugh, thinking she must have misheard.

"Cut the rest of the guys," Frankie said. "I'm going on next."

"Alright," Rachel said. "Are you sure?"

"Yeah, yeah," Frankie said thinking about it for half-a-beat. "Do it."

"If you say so," Rachel said.

Frankie then watched as she walked up to the front of the line and signaled for everyone's attention.

"Hey guys, listen up," she said. "All you guys are cut."

No one in the line moved. They all just looked at each other, confused.

"Get the fuck out!" Frankie yelled in a hushed whisper (he didn't want to ruin the shot). "Go, go, go!" He started shoving the guys out of the line and pointing towards the door.

As the guys cleared out of the garage, Rachel looked out of the curtain to see how the scene was going. Frankie then walked up to her and she looked at him.

"You almost ready to go?" Rachel asked.

"Yes," Frankie said, even though he wasn't actually sure if he was ready or not.

"Alright then…" Rachel said, as she looked back through the curtain. She then waved Frankie through, "Go now."

As soon as Frankie entered the red-curtained

Gangbang Arena everything seemed to start moving in slow motion. His eyes landed on Maxine and his heart couldn't help but break. She looked absolutely haggard.

She was still beautiful, that much was certain (her cum and sweat covered body glistened in the light and she glowed like an angle), but her hair was slick and matted. Her make-up was smeared. She could barely keep her eyes open. To Frankie, it appeared as though something was *off* about her. The Maxine on the cum soaked bed was not the Maxine that Frankie knew and loved.

Time began to move at its normal pace as Frankie rushed to Maxine's side. He put his hand on her sticky face and she looked up at him, delirious from valium and fornication.

"What are you doing here?" Maxine asked with a giggle, as though she'd ran into an old friend she hadn't seen in awhile.

"Come on," Frankie said. "Let's go."

"Where are we going?" Maxine asked.

"We've got to get you out of here," Frankie said as he went to pick her up.

"Okay," Maxine said as she closed her eyes again.

Frankie then hoisted her body up, cradling her. She rested her head on his shoulder. Her skin gripped to his robe.

"Hey," Tony said when he saw it happening from behind the camera he was manning. "Are we done or what?"

"Fuck you, Tony," Frankie said as he turned around, making his way to an exit. "Cut it. All of it. We're done."

"Sure thing, chief," Tony said as he turned to the rest of the camera operators. "Lets cut the cameras guys."

Frankie then made it to the curtain and fumbled with it. Rachel helped him move it; she seemed shocked when she saw Frankie holding Maxine.

"What's going on?" Rachel asked as Frankie hurried by her.

"We're done," Frankie said as he exited the garage.

"I can see that," Rachel could be heard saying before the garage door slammed behind Frankie and Maxine.

Frankie then carried Maxine up the stairs. His arms began to strain a bit; her body was dead weight at that point.

"I'm going to need some help from you, Maxine," Frankie said as he made it halfway up the stairs.

"Huh?" Maxine asked as she tilted her head up to Frankie's.

"Can you, like, hold on to me?" Frankie asked as he hefted her up a bit. "Or else I'm going to have to fireman you up."

"Oh no," Maxine said with a giggle, "don't do that." She then clutched Frankie and the weight she was putting on Frankie's arms let up. "I don't like fires," she added, more seriously.

"I know you don't," Frankie said with a smile.

Frankie thought about putting Maxine in her bed, but she reeked of that sour, papier-mâché smell that cum has. He knew if he were even partially responsible for contaminating her bed with that smell, he would never hear the end of it. Instead, he took her to his bathroom

112

and laid her on the floor. He had just cleaned it so he didn't feel bad about doing this.

He then went to a cupboard and pulled out some towels, which he laid in the tub. Once he had made a little pallet that he thought would be comfortable enough, he filled up the water in the tub.

"I'm on your floor?" Maxine asked, slightly offended.

"Yep," Frankie said. "But it's clean, I promise."

"Gross," Maxine said.

"Alright," Frankie said once the tub had filled up to a reasonable amount. "Let's get in the tub."

"The tub?" Maxine asked as Frankie lifted her up. "The both of us?"

"No," Frankie said. "Just you."

"Okay," Maxine said as she was placed gently onto the towels in the tub in the water. "Oh, that's cold. Can you warm it up?"

"Sure," Frankie said as his hand moved to the faucet. "How much valium did you take?"

"I don't know," Maxine said with a little laugh, "I feel really good though."

"Well that's good," Frankie said as he grabbed a bottle of shampoo and squeezed some out onto his hand. "You seem loose."

"Rude," Maxine said. "Never call a woman loose."

They shared a laugh and Frankie began to massage the shampoo into Maxine's matted, clumpy hair. He tried to be gentle, but some of the cum had began to dry and was holding some strands together like glue.

"Is this what heroin is like?" Maxine asked.

"I don't know," Frankie said. "I haven't done valium, gotten gang-banged and then laid in cold water as it warms up before."

"You should try it," Maxine said. "It has to be close."

Frankie laughed as he worked hard at trying to rid Maxine's hair of jizz.

"What are you doing?" Maxine asked, lying in the tub, moving her hands around in the water like dolphins. Her scalp was too numb to feel any pain, but she could feel Frankie's hands in her hair and it made her feel a little funny.

"I'm washing your hair, Maxy," Frankie said. It dawned on him that he hadn't called her "Maxy" in years. It felt strange to say it, not because it was a foreign word, but because it came out as though he had never stopped calling her that.

"Why are you washing it?" Maxine asked, as Frankie poured water over her hair gingerly, so as to wash the soap out.

"Because there's cum in it," Frankie said.

"Damn, that sucks," Maxine said with a pout.

"I know, I'm sorry," Frankie said as he ran his fingers through her now cleaner hair, trying to get the last little bits of cum out.

"Why?" Maxine asked. "It wasn't you was it?"

"No," Frankie said with a melancholy to his tone. "It was the other guys, those mother-fuckers. We specifically told them to avoid it, too."

"Eh," Maxine said with a shrug. "Boys will be boys."

"More like 'boys will be assholes,'" Frankie said. "I'm

114

sorry Maxine, I really am. I know you didn't want them to do that, and I- I don't know…"

"Don't worry about it, Francis," Maxine said. "If there's one thing I've learned from knowing you, it's how to roll with the punches."

"Yeah…" Frankie said. The melancholy turned to full-blown sorrow and he stood up. He looked down at Maxine with sadness in his eyes. He saw the Maxine of now, the one he'd grown to hate for some reason he couldn't comprehend, and he saw the Maxine of years ago, the one he'd loved with a passion only now reserved for narcotics.

"Where are you going?" Maxine asked, looking up to Frankie.

"I'm going to get you some clothes," he said. "You're all naked and, if I know you, you'll be cold soon."

"That's true," she said with a smile. "Thanks, Francis."

"No problem," Frankie said as he went to the door and opened it. "You should wash the rest of that cum off."

"Alright," Maxine said. "Hurry back."

"Will do," Frankie said and then he walked out.

As soon as Frankie shut the door behind him the melancholy-turned-sorrow turned into something far worse. It became a wretched, awful bleakness that Frankie hadn't felt in a very long time. A black void ripped open inside of him and began to shout and curse and whip at his very soul. It was too much to take and Frankie fell to his knees.

He began to cry. Sobs left his mouth and tears streamed down his eyes. He was positive he had never felt worse than this, ever. The worst hangover he had ever experienced was nothing compared to this. All other pain had been tangible or physical. He could wrap his mind around them. But this horrid feeling wrecked him in a way that would never heal.

All he could do was cry and think about getting high.

*No*, he thought, there on the floor. *Get it fucking together. Get her clothes, then get high.*

"Get her clothes," Frankie repeated aloud, "then get high."

He then rose to his feet, wiped off his tears, and went to Maxine's room to find her something to wear.

---

After Frankie had gotten Maxine all situated, he went to the upstairs living room, where Miles was watching TV and smoking weed. Frankie plopped down on the couch with a sigh. He'd done a few lines of coke and had a shot or two of bourbon, but the effects were leaving much to be desired. It's not that he was having a bad trip or wasn't feeling it, it's that he wanted something *more*. He wanted something that would punch him in the gut or open his mind, maybe at the same time. He didn't know what that was though.

As he pondered what it could be, his eyes drifted to the TV. Miles was watching one of their old movies. Maxine and Rachel were starring in it, and it was one of the first times Frankie had any semblance of production value.

Frankie couldn't remember the plot, but from what he could tell, Maxine is playing a regal lady of some kind and

Rachel is dressed as (what one could only assume) is Maxine's maid. The two of them are feverishly kissing each other as they strip off each other's clothes before they begin sixty-nining. Maxine is on top and is falling victim to Rachel's ravishing tongue work. Rachel is too good. Maxine is too enthralled in the work Rachel is doing to be doing any work herself.

Maxine kneels, sitting on Rachel's face. Rachel begins licking her asshole. Both of them moan.

"This is my favorite part," Miles said as he puffed on a joint.

"Which movie is this?" Frankie asked, not taking his eyes off the close-up of Maxine's O-face.

"Madame Fur Burger and the Temptress of Twats," Miles said with a chuckle.

"Oh yeah," Frankie said. "Maxine was Madame Fur Burger."

"And Rachel was The Temptress," Miles added.

"No, remember?" Frankie asked. "The whole thing was that 'The Temptress' was inside the Madame all along."

"Oh yeah, that's right," Miles said. He then turned back to the screen and watched it as though it instantly mesmerized him. "Man," he said as he watched. "We totally need to do one of these lezzy pictures again."

"No way, man," Frankie said with a laugh, "I'm done with normal shit." Frankie then motions to the joint. "Let me get a hit of that."

Miles looked away from the screen and handed it to Frankie. He watched as Frankie took a long drag.

"So, how's Maxine doing?" Miles asked.

"Good I guess," Frankie said, holding the smoke in. He then exhaled, "She's all out of it."

"It's probably all the valium she took," Miles said.

"Yeah…" Frankie said as he took another puff from the joint and passed it to Miles. Before Miles could take it though, an idea struck Frankie, "I think we need to go to Amsterdam."

"What?" Miles said in amused shock, as he took the joint. "Why?"

"I need new and exciting shit," Frankie said. "Like in every aspect of my life. I also feel like we'd find good shit to work with there. Like weird shit. We could find something that no one here is doing yet. I think Amsterdam is the place to go for something like that. I also think the drugs there would be amazing."

"Alright," Miles said hardly thinking about it. "We'll run it by Maxine when she's back up and running. She'd probably be down to go."

"No," Frankie said, almost harshly. "Absolutely not. I don't want her there."

"Why not?" Miles asked.

"Because I hate her," Frankie answered after he'd thought about it for a while. "Or at least I think I do. Maybe. I don't know. Either way, I think I need some time on my own. I need to do my own shit. She cramps my imagination."

"Sounds valid, I guess," Miles said. "Let's do it."

"Cool," Frankie said, standing up. "I'll go pack."

"Wait, you want to go now?" Miles asked.

"Yes," Frankie said. "The way I see it, it's now or never."

"Fair enough," Miles said as he too stood. "Let me find my passport."

"Oh Madame Fur Burger," Rachel's voice came seductively from the television. "Your tongue is just so magical."

Frankie and Miles looked at it and then each other.

"We should bring Rachel," Frankie said. "We might need her."

"Definitely," Miles said with a smirk.

"Oh yeah," Rachel's voice emitted out of the speakers.

As the guys went to get the real-world Rachel and start packing, the scene on the TV played on:

Rachel is bent over, on all fours as Maxine lies under her and fingers her while her tongue works her clit. Rachel lets out a moan and liquid gushes from her cunt and drenches Maxine's face.

"So, it is true what the wise one has claimed," Rachel says, after she came, and turns around to kiss Maxine on the lips. "You really are The Temptress we've been searching for."

# THE 6<sup>TH</sup> ACT OF
# THE GREATEST PORNO EVER MADE

His name was Frankie Wood and he had found himself in a wheelchair. Between his ass and the seat was one of those inflatable-ring cushions that people with hemorrhoids usually sit on. He was dressed in scrubs and he was high on shroom pills. Not too high, mind you. He had built up a tolerance in the time he'd spent abroad.

But now it was time for him to return home.

One month had passed since they left for Amsterdam and as far as Frankie was concerned, they were returning home valiantly. As they approached their home, though, neither Miles nor Frankie looked very valiant. Miles looked worn out, as though he hadn't slept in days. It was clear he'd been rubbing his eyes a lot and he had a greenish hue to his skin. He did, arguably, look better than Frankie.

Frankie didn't care how he looked, though. All that he cared about was getting home so he could start work on his masterpiece. He wanted to try to be as secretive about it as possible, though. That meant that he was trying to get

Miles to sneak him into the house so that they wouldn't have to run into Maxine.

Frankie had found out as soon as he had turned his cell phone back on (for the first time since they had left the country a month before) that Maxine had left message after message in a shrill tone, showing her anger at everyone but James "abandoning" her.

"I don't feel like being sneaky," Miles said, his tone dead, as he wheeled Frankie up the driveway to their house.

"I don't want to deal with Maxine right now," Frankie said, as though that would change Miles' mind.

"You're going to have to eventually," Miles spat.

"I-" Frankie tried to say.

Miles didn't care what Frankie had to say, though, he just wanted to get home and lay down. He was tired beyond belief. No, worse than tired: depressed.

He punched the code into the keypad by the garage door and it began to open up with a loud creaking sound. It wasn't even halfway up before it could be seen that the garage had been stripped vacant, the set had been torn down and all the other sets had (hopefully) been stored somewhere else and not thrown away.

"What the fuck?" Frankie asked when he saw the empty space.

"I don't know," said Miles as he waited for the door to open, somewhat impatiently.

By the time the door opened fully, and Miles went to push Frankie in, Maxine had stormed out from the house, through the garage door and was stomping up to Frankie and Miles. There was clearly a fire burning inside of her.

"So you fucking beg me, *for years*, to do a goddamn gangbang for you and then, after I agree to do it for some *dumbass* reason, you just up and fucking leave and abandon me without a word *for over a month*?!" Maxine shouted as she walked up to Frankie and looked him square in the eyes. Frankie had forgotten how shrill her voice could get. "I mean, what the fuck guys?"

"Not now," Frankie said, waving his hand. "We've got prep to do."

"Prep? For what?" Maxine asked, eyeing the wheelchair.

"Our next project," Frankie said smugly. "Of course."

Frankie then turned to look up at Miles who looked as though he was either distraught or about to vomit.

"Amsterdam was inspiring," Frankie said with a smirk. "Wasn't it, Smiles?"

"I need to go lie down," Miles said, clearly not earning the new nickname Frankie had given him.

Miles walked out of the garage very quickly. Maxine and Frankie watched after him. Frankie shook his head.

"Some people can't handle Amsterdam," he said, as though that explained Miles' behavior.

"Is he alright?" Maxine asked, turning back to Frankie. "And for that matter, why are you in a wheelchair? And where is Rachel?"

"Rachel said she wanted to stay behind for a little while longer," Frankie said with a shrug. "But if you ask me, she ain't never coming back."

"What?" Maxine responded incredulously. "That

doesn't sound like her at all. What about her and James?"

"I don't know what to tell you," Frankie said, looking at Maxine, dead in the eyes. "She fell in love with it over there. She said to tell you 'hello' and that she'd write you soon. Be sure to check your email."

"You're so full of shit, Frankie," Maxine said, factually.

"No ma'am," Frankie said as he reached to the back of his wheelchair and pulled out a cane. He stood up, wobbling slightly, and supported himself on the cane.

Maxine eyed Frankie's unhealthy state and thought about asking him about it. She knew he would just beat around the bush, so she opted to not play into his bullshit.

"How was the trip?" Maxine asked as she watched Frankie limp to the door.

"I'll tell you about it later," Frankie said. "Right now I've got to start prepping for your next project, it's going to be big."

"What's the 'next big project' then?" Maxine asked.

"It's a surprise for now, my dear Maxine," Frankie said with a smirk. "But I promise that you will be remembered forever and ever. Trust me; it's brilliant."

Frankie tried to hobble off quickly, but it was clear walking caused him pain. Maxine watched after him and noticed that some blood was seeping through his scrub pants.

"What did you do to your ass?" Maxine asked, deciding she couldn't not ask him.

"It's a long, fucking story," Frankie said as he turned around. "Although, could you do me a huge favor? I think I need more bandages. Could you run to Catchpenny's and pick some up? I'd ask Smiles, but he's been a turd lately."

"I'll do it if you tell me what is going on," Maxine said.

"I will when you get back," Frankie said. "Now please, I've got work to do."

Frankie then made his way inside the house leaving Maxine out in the garage by herself. She sighed. She thought about not running the errand for Frankie, but she knew she'd eventually be talked into it. She figured she might as well get it out of the way now.

---

Maxine took her time at the store. She enjoyed shopping and hadn't really done it in awhile. The last time she'd been to the store it was a quick in-and-out. The time before that was the same story. And before that and before that as well. In fact, she couldn't recall the last time that she'd truly shopped.

She had missed it. There was something nice and calming about perusing the goods of the store. Just meandering up and down the aisles, aimlessly. She picked up some pasta and sauce, some chips and some bread. She started craving a PB&J, so she picked up some semi-crunchy peanut butter and apricot jelly. She then picked up an assortment of bandages and gauze for Frankie before heading to the checkout line. It was all in all a pleasant experience.

As she walked to the car, her bags in hand, she wondered if she'd ever really know what happened in Amsterdam. Miles seemed despondent, Frankie was in a wheelchair and Rachel was MIA. It seemed like a complete and utter cluster-fuck. Honestly, though, she felt that maybe it was better to be left in the dark

The more she found out about the Frankie, the less she wanted to know. At least the new Frankie, not the Frankie she had first met, the one that used to go by Francis.

As she drove home she wondered what Francis would say about Frankie if the two of them ever had a chance to meet. Francis would probably hate him. How could she know, though, really? It was just something she thought.

She was going to bring up the idea to Frankie when she was giving him the bandages she'd purchased, but something awful happened.

When Maxine arrived back home, she walked upstairs to Frankie's room but didn't find him there. She searched most of the house before she decided to see if he was with Miles. She went to the door to Miles' room, quickly knocked, but proceeded to open it.

When she fully opened the door to Miles' room she screamed.

"Oh my god!" Maxine exclaimed as she went to Miles, who was hanging, by the neck, in his closet.

Frankie was there. He was just standing and looking at Miles. A look of sadness and of whimsy showed on Frankie's face.

"What happened?" Maxine asked.

"He hung himself," Frankie said, bluntly.

"Oh my god, oh my god," Maxine said as she examined Miles to see if he was possibly still alive.

He wasn't.

126

"Stop being dramatic," Frankie said. "There's nothing we can do."

Maxine turned to give Frankie a mean look for being so crass, but when she looked at him, she saw tears were streaming down his face. Perhaps his numbness was caused by shock or something like that. She couldn't be sure.

She turned back to Miles and saw his face. His eyes bulged and his tongue stuck out. There were claw marks on his neck around the rope. For some reason, there was blood coming from his nose and mouth

"Why is his nose bleeding?" Maxine asked, turning to Frankie.

"I don't know," said Frankie turning away from the scene. "Coke?"

"You know he hated coke," Maxine said.

"Well what, then?" Frankie asked. "Maybe he hit himself when he was clawing at the ropes?"

"Why would he be clawing at the ropes?" Maxine questioned.

"Instant regret? Miles was never good at making the correct decision," Frankie guessed.

"Did you do this Frankie?" Maxine asked, somewhat cautiously, but she needed to be sure.

"How dare you," Frankie said as he began to walk out of the room. "Call an ambulance; I'll hide the drugs and shit."

Maxine watched him as he hobbled out of the room, not looking back. There was something strange about his demeanor, but she couldn't put her finger on it.

"This sucks," Frankie said out loud once he'd made it into the hallway. "This really fucking sucks."

Maxine heard him close the door to his bedroom.

---

The day of the funeral had come quicker than Frankie had expected. He thought that those things took longer to put together, but Miles was ready to be put in the ground by the end of the workweek.

Frankie had completely intended to make an appearance at the funeral (he'd gotten all dressed up in black and everything). There was something about the whole affair, however, that made him stay home.

Honoring Miles shouldn't be done in the way his family intended, with all the black and the flowers in a stupid church. Miles hated the church. So, did Frankie. It was one thing they bonded over at first. Frankie missed those conversations they used to have about the corruption and hypocrisy of the church. He missed a lot about Miles.

Instead of going to the funeral, Frankie thought it would be better to remember Miles through his work. He watched all their early films, the ones Miles shot or directed. Most of them were parodies, but all of them were good, from Snatchmen to The Bigger Lebowski (the titles could've used some work, though). Frankie intended to watch them all, back-to-back.

That's what he was in the middle of doing when Maxine walked into the living room and sat down next to Frankie.

"The first rule of Fuck Club is you don't talk about

Fuck Club," Rachel says on the TV. She is topless and punching her left hand into her right hand in a threatening manner. She stands in a dark, dank basement and is surrounded by various nude males and females.

"You know," Frankie said to Maxine after he'd noticed she'd come in. "I think this is the best idea Miles ever came up with. The parodies, you know?"

"Frankie…" Maxine said with a sadness that Frankie didn't want to hear right then.

"I mean, shit," Frankie cut in, "I know it's all like completely ripping-off something else, but goddamn it was a good idea all around. I mean this one especially. The way he connected all the dots like this. It was fucking brilliant. Genius, even."

"You came up with it," Maxine sighed, it was clear she was putout with Frankie's behavior. "You came up with all of it. Miles just wanted to watch the actual movies, you wanted to remake them as pornos."

"I came up with it?" Frankie asked, taken aback a little bit. He thought about it and then he remembered. "Fuck, I did. Well still, it was Miles' baseline idea that was brilliant."

Frankie grabbed a pack of smokes from the table and lit one up. He offers one to Maxine who declined.

"Why weren't you at the funeral?" Maxine asked.

"I didn't feel like it," Frankie said as he took a drag off the smoke. "You know how Miles felt about funerals and churches. He would've hated it if we had gone. So, I guess it's a good thing we stayed in"

"I went, Frankie!" Maxine said. "And you should have

too; everyone thinks you killed him."

"What? Me?" Frankie asked. "Really?" He almost sounded flattered.

"Yes," Maxine said, seriously. "Really."

Frankie let out a loud laugh at the absurdity of it all. It startled Maxine, who honestly wasn't expecting to hear laughter on the day of a good friend's funeral.

"That's fucking hilarious," Frankie said. "Don't you think so?"

"I don't find it funny," Maxine said.

"I can't believe they'd blame me," Frankie laughed some more. "I mean, if you want to blame someone, blame fucking Amsterdam, man."

Maxine thought about asking about Amsterdam again, but knew that Frankie would just tell her he'd tell her later. Or do something worse. Who knew? Frankie had been acting increasingly erratic since Miles died and Maxine thought it was best to not pry.

Instead, she watched as Frankie popped a handful of pills into his mouth and swallowed them down with a slug from a bottle of whiskey.

"What are those?" Maxine asked, motioning to the little wooden tube that Frankie had poured the pills out of.

"They're like shroom pills," Frankie said as he plucked one from the container and looked at it. "It has ground up shrooms and some other shit in there too. It's supposed to act like shrooms, but I don't know. I can't really feel them."

"You've been tripping shrooms?" Maxine asked.

"Yes," Frankie said. "Consistently… For weeks…"

"That's not good, Frankie," Maxine said as she shook her head in disappointment.

"Well no, not at first." Frankie said. "But once you get to know your hallucinations, everything turns peachy pretty quickly."

With all the "peachiness" he could muster he cut himself a line from the little mound of cocaine on the coffee table. He whistled a little tune as he did this, punctuating the end of the melody with a snort as he sucked the blow up his nose.

Maxine shook her head at Frankie as she watched. She couldn't believe what he'd become. It seemed like it happened quickly. She knew that couldn't be true, but that's how it *seemed*. She did know for sure, he was doing worse more recently.

"What happened in Amsterdam, Frankie?" Maxine couldn't hold it back any longer. She needed to know what made Miles kill himself and Rachel stay. She needed to know what happened to Frankie.

"You know, Maxine," Frankie said, ignoring the question. "We really need to make this next thing that I've been thinking up."

"Frankie!" Maxine shouted, reaching her wits' end. "Will you fucking talk to me?!"

"YOU SHUT YOUR FUCKING MOUTH!" Frankie shouted as he slammed his fist into the table. Cans of beer and an ashtray bounced up or fell over, the white powder shot into the air, coating the table in what looked like snow.

Maxine just froze in place. She had never seen Frankie

have an outburst like that. Sure, he'd thrown tantrums and threatened to kill people, but this was a straight up explosion. It frightened her to see him so volatile. She didn't know what to say.

She didn't have to say anything though because as quickly as the storm came, it left. Frankie exhaled and straightened up in the couch. He went back to smoking his cigarette (which was somehow still lit).

"I just really think we need to get this thing done ASAP, Maxine," Frankie said, calmly, as though he hadn't missed a beat. "I think Miles would have enjoyed it. I'd like to make it for him."

Maxine couldn't think of what to say. She couldn't tell what scared her more, his outburst or how quickly he was able to drop it.

"Please, Maxine?" Frankie said, turning to look at her with sad, puppy-dog eyes. "It would mean a lot."

"Frankie…" Maxine said, trying to buy herself some time, so she could process what was happening. "Yes… We'll do it Frankie. We'll do it for Miles."

"Thank you," Frankie said as he turned back to the TV.

"What is the idea?" Maxine asked, wishing she wouldn't have been too scared to ask before she had agreed.

"Shhh," Frankie said as he pointed at the TV. "Let's talk about it tomorrow. Tonight, can't we just chill?"

"Sure," Maxine said as she looked up to the television to see what Frankie was watching. It was the end of one of their videos.

In it, Frankie fucks Maxine's mouth as she holds her

ankles. Frankie lets out a few pumps and a moan before he pulls out and cums all over her face. She looks up at him and smiles as she wipes the jizz into her mouth and swallows it. Frankie then leans down and kisses her.

Maxine couldn't help, but smile as she watched it. Those were simpler times.

---

It took a few days to set everything up, but Frankie did it. He let Tony help set up the cameras the day of, but wouldn't let him bring on any extra staff. Frankie did the rest of it all himself. He didn't trust anyone else to help. It needed to be just right, it needed to be perfect. It could be the greatest thing he'd ever done, it could be The Perfect Porno. The thing he believed he always sought after.

He didn't want to spoil it, though. He didn't want to tell anyone what his plan actually was. He thought they would ruin it like they always did. In his defense, he was most likely right. Not only would they probably have qualms about the subject matter, but the people he surrounded himself with were dense and incapable of seeing the bigger picture.

It became even more evident when he gathered James and Maxine together on the day of the shoot to explain almost everything to them. They were having trouble trying to wrap their minds around what was going on in Frankie's head.

"Wait, wait, wait," James said, after he'd heard Frankie go through it all once already. "Were you speaking in tongues through half of it? I didn't get a thing you said man. I'm sorry. Could you run it by us one more time, please?"

"You stupid mother-fucker," Frankie said, but before he could go into the plot of what they were about to shoot, again, Tony walked up.

"Hey, chief," Tony said. "Camera's are all set. What's going on over here?"

"This is an up and down conversation," Frankie said. "It'd be right if you left." Frankie smirked as he turned back to James and Maxine.

"Why are you always such a dick to me?" Tony asked.

"Fuck you, Tony," Frankie responded. "It's 'cause you're a fucking dolt."

"It's not right, man," Tony said.

"Really Tony? You want to pick this time to take a stand?" Frankie asked with an angry laugh. "Right fucking now? Right before we're doing shit? I'll fucking kill you tonight, mother-fucker."

"I'm sorry, man," Tony said, "I was just trying to let you know I was done with the cameras."

"Well go fucking check them again," Frankie said as he shooed Tony off. He then turned back to James and Maxine. "Where were we?"

"You were going to tell us your nonsensical plot again," Maxine said, clearly feeling a little loopy from some muscle relaxers she'd taken in preparation for the scene (at Frankie's insistence).

"Don't get snippy," Frankie said. "That's my job, alright?"

"Sorry," Maxine said. "Those muscle relaxers are

kicking in; I just want to go lie down."

"Alright, fine," Frankie said. "I'll make it quick: Basically it's the story of a quadriplegic nymphomaniac (hence why Maxine's on loads of muscle relaxers) and James is going to play her lover. It needs to be sexy and intimate with a lot of real passion. I'm going to need to see some real love between you two."

"I don't think I can do that with Maxine," James said, before turning to Maxine apologetically. "I don't mean any offense."

"Oh, none taken, big guy," Maxine said, sarcastically.

"Why can't you do it, James?" Frankie asked.

"I just can't be intimate with people I don't feel that way about. I could fuck her, sure. But I don't know if I can *make love*," James said. "Why can't we just wait for Rachel to come back?"

"For the last fucking time," Frankie said, "Rachel probably won't be coming back. And to top that off, every one of our customers loves Maxine to death. Even more so now that we've hinted that she's coming out of retirement."

"I know all that," James said like he'd heard it a million times. "But Rachel said in her last email she might be coming back."

"Dude," Frankie said with as much sympathy as he could muster. "Look James, you weren't there, man. She fucking loved it there. I mean shit, I would've stayed if I could've. So let's just get over Rachel, okay? Now, where was I?"

"You were saying something about me and James

trying to be in love or something," Maxine said, slowly blinking.

"Oh yeah," Frankie said, before he tried to brush passed the next part. "And there's going to be a twist at the end."

"And what's this 'twist' you're talking about?" Maxine asked.

"Now that, Maxine," Frankie said, "is a surprise."

"What, dude? No," James said. "I'm not going to do something if I don't know what it is."

"It's not going to be a secret to you, James," Frankie said condescendingly. "Just to Maxine."

"What?" Maxine asked. "Why me?"

"Because I'm going to need your performance to be believable," Frankie said. "Speaking of, how're you feeling pill-wise?"

"Loose as a goose, baby," Maxine said with a laugh. "Woo!" she exclaimed while she lifted her hands up victoriously and almost fell over as she did so.

"Awesome," Frankie said before he waved to Tony. "Hey Tony, be useful- will you? -and walk Maxine to her bed please?"

"Yeah, sure," Tony said as he walked over to Maxine and helped her stand up straight. The two of them walked off.

Frankie watched them as they walked off. He made sure they were out of earshot before he turned back to James.

"So, what's the deal with this twist, man?" James asked.

136

Frankie looked back over to Tony and Maxine, as she was helped onto the bed.

"You know what?" Frankie said. "I think we should have this conversation in my office."

"You're office?" James asked.

"My bedroom, you dumb fuck," Frankie said.

Frankie then ushered James out of the garage and up to his room. He was glad his room was a little bit of a walk from the garage. He needed to think about the things he was going to tell James. It all had to be worded perfectly. If it wasn't, it could ruin things. The last thing he wanted was for things to be ruined before they even got started.

He popped two shroom pills as they walked into the room and shut the door behind them. He smiled at James in an almost wicked manner.

"So, what's the twist, man?" James asked as Frankie led him to the middle of the room.

"Look James," Frankie said as he thought about the best way to break the news to James, "I've got to come clean with you…"

He then let out a faux-sorrowful sigh to add an aura of drama to the situation. *This is going to be good*, Frankie thought. *This is going to be so fucking good.*

# THE 7<sup>TH</sup> ACT OF
# THE GREATEST PORNO OF ALL TIME

His name was Frankie Wood and he'd never been to Amsterdam before, but almost as soon as he landed he felt like he was home. The weather was nice, the women were beautiful and the drinks on the flight had been completely free and damn near bottomless.

"So, what should we do first?" Miles asked as they walked off the airplane.

"We could knock the Anne Frank House out first, yeah?" Rachel suggested.

"Jesus Christ, Rachel," Frankie said. "If I wanted to get bummed out at a girl's childhood home I'd go back home to Maxine's."

"We could check out The Van Gogh Museum," Miles said with a shrug.

"Are you guys serious?" Frankie asked. "We're in fucking Amsterdam. We're going to get fucked up as quickly as possible. Do you think it's easy to get a hotel around here?"

"I don't know," Miles said, "I'll go ask around."

Miles then walked off, towards the taxi area, leaving Rachel and Frankie standing there in the middle of the hustle and bustle of the airport.

"Are you okay, Frankie?" Rachel asked. "You seem a little on edge."

"I'm just depressed," Frankie said, shrugging. "I just need a little bit of a vacation, I think. I feel like I'm going insane. I'm just doing the same thing over and over and over again, and expecting new shit to happen, you know what I mean?"

"I don't know," Rachel said. "I like what we do. We're pretty lucky, you know? I mean we just have sex and do drugs all day and we get paid for it. Like *paid*-paid. Paid enough to come to Amsterdam on a whim with no plan. You've got to admit that's pretty awesome, right?"

"Yeah, there's no doubt it's awesome," Frankie concurred. "But don't you ever feel vacant? Don't you ever feel like there's this hole in you that needs to be filled?"

"Yep, all the time," Rachel said, before she winked and playfully nudged Frankie. "But that's what James' dick is for." She then saw that Frankie didn't laugh at her joke. "Oh come on, that was funny."

"It was," Frankie said as he feigned a laugh, "but you've got to know what I mean, right? Like, I need something *more* than all of this. That's all I've ever really wanted."

"Well maybe you just need to do something other than work and drugs all the time?" Rachel suggested. "You should pick up a hobby or something. Oh! I know! You should get a girlfriend or something. Like a real one, not just one of the girls you film."

"I don't want a girlfriend," Frankie said, not wanting to continue the conversation any longer, "I just… I feel like that's the last thing I need."

"No," Rachel said. "It's that last thing you *want*."

"What's that supposed to mean?" Frankie asked, slightly offended.

"You know what it means," Rachel said. "It seems like you go out of your way to avoid that kind of thing. And I think you know why."

"Why?" Frankie said, really not knowing the answer.

"Because you're still all into Maxine, you big dummy," Rachel chided (as any friend would).

"Oh come on," Frankie said with a laugh. "That's not true."

"You know it is, Frankie," Rachel said. "I mean think about it; you'll find it obvious."

"I really don't see it," Frankie said after giving it half-a-thought.

"That's ridiculous," Rachel said. "It's true. I mean shit, man. You remember when we were doing our thing-whatever it was? All you ever talked about was Maxine. You called me her name while we fucked a few times. You've called loads of girls her name. Don't you remember having to cut it out of stuff? It happened like all the time. *All of the time*. It was actually a bit of a joke. Ask Miles when he gets back."

"Oh yeah," Frankie said remembering it with a

grimace, "I forgot about that. Shit, man, I guess you're right."

"I'm always right, Frankie," Rachel said with a playful smirk. "Don't you forget that."

"Jesus, fuck," Frankie said, "I really had no idea I was letting this get to me. Shit- I'm so sorry, Rachel"

"Don't sweat it," Rachel said. "You've shown me a wonderful life."

"Hey guys," Miles said as he walked up, parting the crowd as he did so.

"Let's talk about this later," Frankie whispered to Rachel as Miles reached them.

"Alright," Rachel whispered back.

"So," Miles began, "my whatever they speak here- is it Danish? Dutch? -is rusty, but I think I got us a cab that will take us to a nice hotel in their artsy district."

"Sweet man," Frankie said as he grabbed his bag. "Where's it at?"

"This way," Miles said as he began to lead them towards the taxi area.

Rachel and Frankie followed him as best they could. For some reason Miles was walking quickly.

"Hey," Frankie said. "Do you think you could slow down a little?"

"Sure, sorry," Miles said as he let up the pace. "I'm just in a hurry to find one of those weed cafes. I hear they are beyond compare."

"Yeah," Frankie said. "Do you think they sell those shroom pills?"

"You want to do shrooms?" Rachel asked.

142

"Well it's mixed with other stuff," Frankie said. "It's supposed to be a different high. Like the mindfulness of shrooms with the whatever the fuck from the other shit."

"Sounds like you've done your research," Rachel said.

"It sounds fun," Frankie said with a shrug

"I'll pass, thank you," Rachel said. Then, remembering the multiple Jack and Gingers from the plane ride over, she added, "I could use another drink, though."

"Me too," Frankie agreed. "Miles, where the fuck is this guy?"

"Uh…" Miles said as he looked around the cab area. He then saw the driver he was looking for and waved to him. "There he is! That's the guy."

Frankie and Rachel looked at each other when they saw the guy who was supposed to drive them. He looked skeevy and it wasn't even apparent that his car was a taxi.

"Are you sure this guy is legit?" Frankie asked.

"Yeah," Rachel added. "He looks sketchy."

"He's fine," Miles said, "I mean, you know, let's live a little. We're on fucking vacation guys."

"Eh," Frankie said, before he agreed. "Touché."

He and Rachel then shrugged at each other and followed Miles towards the cab. They smiled and shook hands with the driver. They then got in the car and let it take them to a very nice hotel.

---

The week and a half that had passed them by had been, at least to two of them, a complete and utter waste of time. All they had done was get drunk or high, or, rather, watch

Frankie get drunk and high. It had gotten so bad that both Rachel and Miles had actually wanted to try to get some work done. For some reason though, Frankie wasn't having it.

Recently, he had gotten a taste for absinthe and had been trying to find "the perfect shot" around the city. He had sworn, many times, that he had found it, but at that moment (like many before) he was being very adamant that he was now holding the best one in his hand.

He lifted the shot of absinthe to the middle of the table of the nice little bar they had found themselves in.

"To Amsterdam!" Frankie said, for what had to be the hundredth time.

"To Amsterdam!" Rachel and Miles said with as little enthusiasm as possible.

They all then clinked their glasses and watched as Frankie downed his shot. He then motioned for the barkeep to bring him another almost instantaneously.

"Now this is absinthe, right?" Frankie said, nodding his head in agreement with himself.

"Sure, man," Miles said, trying to amuse Frankie.

"It tastes like everywhere else," Rachel said, clearly done amusing Frankie.

"No," Frankie argued. "They prepare it differently here, I can taste it. Your pallet just isn't sophisticated, yet."

"Yeah," Rachel said as she rolled her eyes. "So Frankie, do you think we're going to get work done today?"

"Work, work, work," Frankie said in a condescending tone. "That's all you two think about."

144

"I thought that is what we were supposed to be doing here," Rachel said. "Or was I mistaken about the purpose of this trip?"

"Yeah man," Miles agreed. "When you asked us to come you said we were going to find something new to shoot. I mean sure, you also said we were going to party a little bit, but this has gotten a little out of hand, don't you think? Like all we've done is go to different bars, cheers to Amsterdam and carry your ass home when you're done."

"Seriously?" Frankie asked as he shook his head in disbelief. "That's how you see this? All of this?"

"Yes," Miles said without a thought.

"Definitely," Rachel concurred.

"Man," Frankie said, his feelings obviously offended. "Fuck the both of you, alright? It just doesn't work like that. We can't just go and find inspiration. Inspiration finds you. You've just got to sit and wait for it. When it comes-"

"You gave us this speech yesterday," Rachel cut in.

"Yeah," Miles added. "And the day before that too."

"Well obviously you two aren't capable of understanding," Frankie said. "I mean don't you remember how all of this shit started? Don't you remember how we got here? I mean, fuck, don't you ever think of the good ol' days? Remember how we used to just get ideas and make shit up? We'd all sit around- you guys, me, Maxine - and shit would just come to us and we'd shoot it. We'd do parodies, we'd do original stuff, weird fetish things, whatever, but we'd never *just* do them. They'd have to come to us first, and do you guys remember how we used to come up with those ideas? Drugs! Booze! Different Drugs! More Booze! Repeat it over and over and over again until something popped into our dumbass heads. And I didn't hear you guys complaining then. Half the time you were in the bathroom cutting up lines for me, Rachel. Those were great times. Better times than this. What the fuck happened to those times? I loved those times. I used to be happy then, but now all I get is two sticks in something that looks like mud but definitely smells like shit."

"Frankie…" Miles began to say as he stared at Frankie like he had tuned him out for half the story, "I don't think I ever remember you being happy. It was never really like that, man."

"Well," Rachel chimed in, "the drugs in the bathroom part is true."

"Well that aside," Miles said, "the rest is bullshit. I used to grab the camera and film your ideas. You would've just preferred to get high and ignore all the other stuff, exactly like you're doing now. You used to have us there to push you. The only thing that's changed is that you've stopped listening to us."

"Well, yeah," Frankie said, realizing he might have misspoken and tried to think of a way to remedy it. "I wasn't saying that was *exactly* how it used to be, alright? I was saying that that is how it *could* be if you just chilled the fuck out and let me do my thing. Everything could've been way easier."

"Wait, wait, wait," Miles said, sipping his absinthe. "You're saying *that* is what your point was?"

146

"I didn't get that at all," Rachel added.

"Well that's what I meant," Frankie said, defensive as always.

"It sure did seem like you were talking about how it used to be," Rachel said.

"How it used to be? How it should be? What's the difference?" Frankie asked as the barkeep brought his newly prepared absinthe.

Frankie shot the drink down.

"It seems like the difference should be pretty obvious," Rachel said sarcastically.

"No ma'am," Frankie said as he shook his head and patted down his pockets. "Now where them pills at?"

Rachel sighed as she reached into her purse and pulled out a little wooden container of pills. She handed it to Frankie who took it with the enthusiasm of a child getting candy.

"I think you should stop taking those pills," Miles said. "I heard prolonged usage can make you go insane or something."

"Oh, is that so?" Frankie giddily asked as he poured some pills into his hand and threw them into his mouth, washing them down with Rachel's barely-drank absinthe.

"I think Miles is right," Rachel said, "I think they're affecting your mind."

"I didn't ask for your opinion," Frankie said, sounding a little harsher. "Either way, the only things these pills affect is my shits. Oh- speaking of my shits; have we tried the herring here yet?"

"Dude," Miles said, "I'm serious. I think those pills are

getting to you. I mean it seems like you can't keep your thoughts together."

"Jesus Christ, man," Frankie said. "The pills help me think. You guys are sounding like fucking Maxine."

"Well someone has to be Maxine," Rachel said, "she's the only one you'll listen to."

"That's not true," Frankie said before he turned to Miles. "Is that true?"

"Yeah, man," Miles said. "She's the only one who can corral you."

"I think she should have come," Rachel added.

"What the fuck did you say?" Frankie asked in a perturbed manner.

"I said," Rachel condescended, "Maxine should have come, she's the only one who seems to be able to keep your ass in check."

Frankie slammed his fist down on the table.

"No!" Frankie shouted. "We don't need Maxine, god damn it. She doesn't control anything or anyone or whatever you said. She just constricts my imagination and pisses on all our parades."

"At least we'd be getting work done," Rachel retorted. "Shit, we'd probably be home by now."

"Shit man," Frankie said, gesturing for another order of three absinthes with his hand, "again with the fucking work. Can't you just enjoy it here?"

"No," Rachel said, "I can't. This place fucking sucks a James-sized dong. I hate it here. Why couldn't we go to France or Budapest or something? I hear Zlovya is Europe's secret hotspot right now."

"Because," Frankie explained, "France and Budapest don't have a plethora of nasty-ass brothels to rip-off ideas from and I have no idea what or where Zlovya is."

"So, when are we going to these 'nasty-ass brothels' then?" Rachel asked.

"Yeah, man," Miles added. "All we've done is talk about it. Don't you think we should get around to seeing what's up with them sooner rather than later?"

"Yes?" Frankie said, unsure of how to respond to Miles' question, which didn't really seem like a question to him.

"Then why aren't we at one right fucking now?!" Rachel raised her voice a bit.

"Fuck you," Frankie said, raising his tone to meet Rachel's. "No need to fucking yell, damn it! We'll get there when we get there!" He was close to causing a scene.

"Hey now," Miles said, trying to diffuse the situation. "Let's all calm down, alright? It was just a suggestion."

"A suggestion, eh?" Frankie said thinking about it. "Hmm... Alright, then..."

As Frankie continued to think about it, the barkeep came by with three more absinthes.

"Okay," Frankie said as he eyed the glasses in front of him, "I've got a suggestion for you two. How about we take these here shots- maybe have a few more -and then, when we're done here, we hit up some brothels you guys are so keen on."

Frankie then turned to Miles for approval of his proposition.

"Sounds good to me," Miles said as he grabbed his absinthe.

"How about you, worker-bee?" Frankie said, turning to Rachel and pushing her glass towards her.

"That's fine with me," Rachel said as she lifted her drink.

"Good," Frankie said, raising his glass and motioning for Miles to do the same. "Alright, on three: One, Two, Three:"

"To Amsterdam!" They all said as they clinked their glasses and downed their drinks.

Frankie then ordered another round and another one.

They didn't wind up going to the brothel that night. Instead, it turned out to be like all the other nights they'd had there. Frankie got drunk and loopy and Miles carried him home while Rachel complained the whole time.

---

Frankie had a dream that night, which was strange for him. He rarely dreamt. Or at least he rarely remembered them. Perhaps he wasn't sleeping well or perhaps it was bullshit that everyone dreamed. It didn't matter, though, he could have had a dream every single night, but the one he had that night would still have made him feel just as strange.

It involved Frankie and the gang all waiting in the green room of an old theatre. Apparently they were all in a band and they were moments away from going on. Frankie was nervous, his hands were sweating and his heart was racing. He sat in the corner, away from the rest of the guys.

Rachel and James were sitting on the couch, heavily

flirting with one another. Miles sat near them, listening to headphones and miming playing the drums. Tony was there too, for some reason, but he was dressed like a roadie, so that's probably what he was.

Then there was Maxine.

She was sitting there, staring into a mirror with light bulbs framing it, seemingly lost in her own thoughts. Frankie was staring at her. He couldn't help it. He felt a sorrow in him as he did so. Also there was a longing he couldn't quite place at first. Something was missing between them and he didn't know what it was. All he knew was that he missed it.

Maxine looked up and the two of them made eye contact. She smiled at Frankie and Frankie looked away. Soon, though, Maxine walked over to him and sat beside him.

"You doing alright?" Maxine asked. "You look miserable."

"I don't think so," Frankie said. "I'm just nervous."

"Oh come on, now," Maxine said, "You don't think I can see through that? I think I know what's up. Do you want to talk about it?"

"Well," Frankie said as he looked around the room. Everything had fallen quiet and everyone was looking at the two of them. "Yeah, a little bit. But can we do it somewhere more... *private?*"

"Sure thing," Maxine said as she stood and put her hand out for Frankie to take. "Come on."

Frankie took her hand and was led by her to the hallway. They closed the green room door and stood there. An awkward silence overtook them.

"Well?" Maxine asked. "What's going on in that beautiful brain of yours?"

"It doesn't feel beautiful at the moment," Frankie said with a pathetic scoff.

"Well it doesn't have to be beautiful all the time," Maxine said in a comforting manner. "What's going on with you?"

"I'm just-" Frankie said trying to find the words before he met Maxine's eyes. "Why did you break up with me?"

"Frankie," Maxine said, "I had no idea it still effected you. It was years ago. I thought we moved passed it."

"*You* moved passed it," Frankie said with a little scorn. "It's all I can think about."

"Then why is this the first time I'm hearing about it?" Maxine asked.

"I don't know," Frankie said with a shrug. "It was like when you broke up with me, we were on a train together, and instead of dealing with it, I just fell asleep. I slept for the whole ride and then the end of the line came and I got woken up and you were gone. The end of the line is now, Maxine. I just woke up and I feel like shit."

"Damn," Maxine said, "I had no idea."

"I know," Frankie said, "All I can think about is how nothing lasts. And I'm supposed to write and sing love songs now. There's thousands of people out there wanting to hear my words. How am I supposed to sing to them? Love has lost all meaning."

"Look, Frankie," Maxine said as she put her hand on Frankie's shoulder. "You and me were in a storm. The

152

storm raged and was wild and lightening crashed and thunder boomed. It was great, but I wanted to stay inside and just watch the storm. You wanted to run out there like a child. You wanted to get struck by lightening to see what if felt like. It was like you had a death wish."

"Maybe I did," Frankie said, "I don't know. I know I've been crazy with the coke and the sex and the booze- well not the booze, but everything else -but it's all been because I am like an ocean and you were like my salt. Did you know that without the salt, all the animals in the sea would die? That's how all this feels to me; everything in me is dying."

"You have been going a little crazy," Maxine agreed.

"I know," Frankie said, a little ashamed. "But it's just my head has been stuck in a vice and shit is squeezing in and in an in and it hurts. And then I have fucking Miles and Rachel giving me advice about you, but I don't want to hear it. I just want to do drugs. That's the only thing that fills the void in my heart you left."

"I'm sorry, Frankie," Maxine said, not sounding overly sincere.

"Look," Frankie said, "it's clear you don't really care and that I'm just burdening you with this shit. You don't have to pretend you do. You can head back in, I just need a minute."

"No, Frankie, it's good," Maxine said. "I'm glad we're finally talking about this."

"Are you, really?" Frankie asked.

"Yes, I am," Maxine said. "There's a lot I've wanted to get off my chest."

"Like what?" Frankie asked.

"Well," Maxine said, thinking about how to word what she wanted to say, "I guess the reason I broke up with you was because I felt we were waiting around for something real to happen, you know? I just felt like I was getting older and wasting away and we weren't doing anything. You were doing your stuff, I was just watching. And before I knew it you were just kind of hurting yourself with your behavior, especially towards me. You loved me too much, you know?"

"Too much?" Frankie said with a laugh. "How the fuck is that even possible?"

"It was like you were worshipping me," Maxine said. "But in an awful way. Like how you are with drugs. You were just with me because I was an idol, not because I was someone you wanted to be with. I mean, don't get me wrong, it was nice at first, but the more you loved me the more you actually pushed me away."

"Sorry," Frankie said. "I'd never been in love before. I didn't think I'd be able to love anyone else as much. I wanted to love everything about you."

"It suffocated me," Maxine said. "Surely you know that. It wasn't fun anymore."

"No," Frankie said. "*This* shit isn't fun. None of this is; fucking working with you, missing you while you're right in front of me, having to sing these stupid fucking love songs that are all about you. You know what's sad? I write parts for you to sing, lovey-dovey shit, just so that I can hear you say them. Because I want you to say them. How pathetic is that?"

"Honestly," Maxine said, trying to turn a joke, "I think it's *very* pathetic."

Frankie had to laugh at that; it was rather funny.

"Look," Frankie said, "I laid my heart on the line, I know I did, and I understand if you don't ever want to see me again. But honestly, that's going to be what needs to happen. You either have to give me another chance or you've got to get out of my life."

"Are you firing me if I don't take you back?" Maxine asked. "Because that's kind of fucked up."

"No, no, no," Frankie said, shaking his head. "But our relationship is just going to strictly have to be work-related from this point forward."

"Okay," Maxine said, "I…"

"What?" Frankie asked, wanting her to finish.

"Guys," Miles said as he opened the door, interrupting their moment.

"What's up, Miles?" Frankie asked, more than a little annoyed.

"They just called for us on the intercom," Miles said, feeling the tension. "We're supposed to make our way up to the stage."

"Ugh, fine," Frankie said to Miles before turning to Maxine. "Look, can we finish this later?"

"Sure," Maxine said as she looked down.

Frankie felt very dissatisfied as the rest of the band walked out of the room and started going down the hall towards the stage. As he followed them, a nagging feeling began to well up inside of him. Suddenly, an idea struck him. He needed to take a stand. He couldn't let that conversation be the end of it. He had to do something grand.

He thought about what he was going to do as they waited to be introduced to the stage.

"Ladies and gentlemen," the announcer said, "let's give a round of applause for Frankie & The Woodies!"

Applause came from the audience as they walked out. Frankie made it to his mark and grabbed his guitar. He then turned to the band, who were waiting on his sign to start. Instead he did something else.

"So," Frankie said into the microphone, "I want to try something different tonight. I'm going to perform a song for you guys that I just wrote. It's going to just be me, so please bear with me."

He then turned to the band with a reassuring look in his eyes. His gaze rested on Maxine.

"This one's for you," he said, then he turned to the audience.

He then played and sang the most beautiful song that had ever been written. It flowed out of him spontaneously and his fingers moved freely. The words came from deep, deep inside of him and he honestly didn't even know what he was saying. He finished with a flourish and faced Maxine at the end and saw she had tears in her eyes.

"I love you," Frankie said.

She approached him and hugged him. She held his face and kissed him.

"That was a masterpiece," she said.

"It was for you," Frankie said.

"I know," Maxine said.

"I love you."

"I love you too."

And then Frankie woke up.

It took him a moment to get his bearings. The memory of the hotel room and why he was there washed over him. He looked around the room and saw Rachel and Miles there, playing some card game on Miles' bed.

"Well look who's up," Rachel said, not looking up from her cards.

"The beast has woken," Miles said.

"Guys," Frankie said, his breath still labored from the horrible dream he'd had, "I just had the craziest dream."

"It's those fucking pills, man," Miles said.

"No," Frankie said, "it wasn't like that, it kind of showed me what I need to do."

"And what do you need to do?" Rachel asked, clearly disinterested.

"Go to a god-damn brothel," Frankie said.

Before Rachel or Miles could respond, Frankie shot up and went to the bathroom to get ready.

---

Frankie had needed a few absinthes before they went to the brothel and *a few* had turned into *a lot*. Needless to say, he was damn near useless by the time they walked into the red-tinted place. Well Frankie didn't "walk," per se. Miles had to carry him in, because Frankie's feet weren't working at one hundred percent.

Miles brought Frankie up to the counter of the brothel.

It was manned (or womanned, as it were) by a very tall blonde woman who was dressed in the garb that one would associate with a dominatrix. She had what one could call "resting bitch face," and her naturally yellow hair was pulled back into a slick ponytail, one that looked like it had just been freshly wetted.

As Miles brought Frankie up, Frankie tripped on his own feet and almost took Miles out during his fall. Rachel rolled her eyes. The woman behind the counter let out a little laugh, breaking character.

"Man, Smiles" Frankie said as he straightened himself. "You are really fucked up."

"Did you just call him 'Smiles'?" Rachel asked, hardly being able to hold in a laugh herself.

"What?" Frankie asked, not sure of what he was doing at that point.

"I heard you call Miles 'Smiles'," Rachel said. "I swear I heard it. Did you mean to do that?"

"No," Frankie said, turning to Miles as best he could. "What is she talking about? Did I call you 'Smiles'?"

"I don't know," Miles said.

"I'm pretty sure you did," Rachel said, turning to the blonde woman behind the counter. "Didn't he?"

"You did," the blonde woman said, pointedly.

"Oh fuck," Frankie said with a laugh, "I must have then. Why the fuck have we never thought of that before?"

"I don't know," Miles said, shaking his head.

"Man," Frankie said, "that's what I'm calling you from now on. You are now known as Smiles."

"Sounds good, man," Miles said.

"Can I help you all?" The blonde woman asked behind the counter in a heavy Dutch accent.

"Yes," Frankie said, straightening himself up as though he was stone cold sober. "We are looking for the- how do you say? -Madame?"

"I am the Madame," the blonde woman said, clearly the Madame.

"Oh, shit," Frankie said. "So you are, my apologizes. How are you doing tonight?"

"I am well," the Madame said, clearly not wanting to deal with more tourists. "What can I help you with?"

"Well," Frankie said, "first off, I wanted to say 'Hi,' to you."

"Well, 'Hello,' then," the Madame said, rubbing the bridge of her nose.

"Great!" Frankie said, taking charge of the awkward situation he had built. "I have some questions for you also."

"Well what are your questions?" the Madame asked.

"Well," Frankie said, trying to choose his words wisely, "I just wanted to know what the weirdest shit we could do here was."

"You want weird *shit*?" The Madame asked, clearly not fully understanding what Frankie meant by "shit."

"He wants to do weird *things*," Rachel tried to clarify. "Like stuff that normal people don't ask for."

"Oh, '*things*,'" the Madame said, "I understand. We have lots of those here."

"Like what?" Frankie asked with a smirk.

159

"Well let's see..." the Madame said, thinking about what she had to offer. "We've got BDSM and pegging."

"No, no, no," Frankie protested, awkwardly. "We need something more than that."

"*Shiza*?" the Madame asked.

"No," Frankie said. "Not that.   I mean I'm not opposed, but we can do that shit- no pun intended -back where we come from.  I want something that is new and exciting, do you know what I mean?"

The Madame rolled her eyes.  She was clearly sick of having to deal with all of it.  To her, it was all stupid bullshit. Just tourist nonsense.

"I'm serious," Frankie said, seeing her eye-roll.

"Oh," the Madame said, with an I-can-fuck-with-this-guy-smirk, "well that kind of thing- how do you say? - costs."  She then moved her main fingers against her thumb in a manner that denoted that she was talking about cash.

"Well," Frankie said, "I just want you to know that money is no issue for us.  Or me.  Whatever works for you."

"Well," the Madame said, sheepishly enough for Frankie to not pick up on it, "if money is no issue, then I have no problem telling you.  Although, I must say, this thing I'm about to offer is *very special*."

"Ah," Frankie said, picking up what she was seemingly putting down, "I think I understand.  I just want you to know that you can trust us."

He then looked to Miles and Rachel and they nodded. He also nodded before he looked back to the Madame.

"We can keep a secret," Frankie said in almost a whisper. "We're good at that kind of thing."

"Well," the Madame said, "if you really can keep a secret…"

"Oh, we can," Frankie reassured.

"What is it?" Miles asked, not being able to hold in his curiosity any longer.

"I don't know if you can handle it," the Madame said, in clearer English than she let on she knew. "It will change you forever."

"We can handle it," Frankie said, buying in to her sales-pitch. "We can handle anything. The only caveat that I have is that I'm not wearing a condom."

"That won't be a problem," the Madame said as she laughed. "It just needs to be kept a secret."

"We'll do whatever you ask, Madame," Frankie said. "Just tell us what it is."

"Okay," the Madame said, leaning in. "It's a thing we do only here, and it's called *snijden*."

"*Snijden*," Frankie said with a laugh. "That sounds perfect."

"I think," the Madame said with a smirk. "It's just what you're looking for."

"Me too," Frankie said. "That's just what we're looking for."

"Okay," the Madame said. "Then who will do it?"

Frankie took that question with the heft it warranted. He looked to Rachel and then Miles.

"Can she do it?" Frankie asked, pointing to Rachel.

"No," the Madame said. "This is a only-man thing."

"Okay," Frankie said before he turned to Miles. "So you or me?"

"Rock, paper, scissors?" Miles asked.

"Yeah," Frankie said. "Go on 'shoot.'"

Frankie and Miles set up in the *rock, paper, scissors* formation. Their fisted hands were in their non-fisted ones. They were ready (and excited) to play.

"Rock, paper, scissors, shoot!" both of them said simultaneously as they hit their fists on their open palms, before- when "shoot!" was said -they picked their respective choices.

Frankie picked rock.

Miles picked scissors.

Frankie laughed in triumph. He was excited to have won.

"Fuck yeah," Frankie said, pumped-up beyond belief.

"Best two out of three?" Miles asked, bummed that he lost.

"Fuck you, Smiles," Frankie said with a smile before he turned to the Madame, "I will do the *snijden!*"

"Very good," the Madame said. "It will cost two-thousand dollars, *Amerikaans.*"

"Fuck," Frankie said, "that seems like a lot."

"Price is all inclusive," the Madame said, as though those words had coaxed a lot of tourists in the past. She didn't really know what they meant, but she said them just the same.

"Well shit," Frankie said with a laugh, clearly understanding what the Madame did not, "for that price, it better be."

"Frankie," Rachel chimed in, "I don't know about this. It sounds weird."

"It is weird," Frankie said, "that's the point."

"I-" Rachel tried to interject.

"No," Frankie said, putting his hand to Rachel's mouth before he turned to the Madame. "Is it worth it?"

"It is worth it," the Madame said with a nod. "I assure you. Nothing else like this."

"See?" Frankie said to Rachel. He then spoke with the Madame. "Is it cool if we film? We'll pay extra."

"*Nee!*" the Madame exclaimed. "No film!"

"Okay, okay, jeez," Frankie said, trying to play off the Madame's strange insistence. He then turned to Rachel. "Give me the wallet."

"Here," Rachel said as she pulled out the wallet from her purse and handed it Frankie.

Frankie took the wallet from Rachel and opened it. He put the cash he took from it on the counter in front of the Madame.

The Madame took the bills in her hand and began to count them, so that she could make sure the whole two thousand was there.

"We good?" Frankie asked after he was sure the Madame had counted the money.

"We're good," the Madame said before she walked away from the counter and motioned towards a doorway. "Right this way."

As she said this, Frankie couldn't help but notice that she pocketed the money in a greedy fashion. Frankie didn't think that this was a strange thing, but the rest of his group did. He couldn't be bothered with it, though. He was far too excited to care about things like that. All he could focus on was the fact that things were shiny and new.

"I'm going to go *snijden*, whatever that is," Frankie said as he turned to Rachel and Miles with a cheese-ball smile.

Both Rachel and Miles shook their heads, as though they meant Frankie to realize he shouldn't do what he was about to do. Frankie ignored their headshakes and followed the Madame.

The Madame led Frankie from the "lobby" and through a corridor, which was filled with door-upon-door of the type of closed-door shenanigans that one would expect. At least, that's what the sounds coming from them would lead one to assume.

"Oh yeah," Frankie said as he walked down the corridor, rubbing his hands together in excited anticipation, "this is what I was expecting when I came to Amsterdam."

"Well, maybe," the Madame said as she continued to lead the way, "you should expect more."

"Yes, yes, yes," Frankie said as he was lead down the corridor. "That is exactly what I was expecting to hear."

All the Madame did was smile when she heard that. She continued to lead Frankie down the hall, passed all the moaning rooms. None of what could be heard was for him. She had something else in mind. He would get what he paid for, and then some.

The Madame's smile continued as she led him to the end of the hallway, the place where she sent all patrons that demanded something more. The door she led him to was the place for *snijden*.

She opened the door, and led Frankie in first.

The room Frankie entered was redder than any room he had ever been in. Before he made note of anything else, he looked up to the red bulb that was hanging from the single light fixture. He seemed to be mesmerized by the aura it was exuding.

"Oh yeah," Frankie said, "I'm feeling this."

He then looked around the room and noticed that there was a bed in the middle of it all. He looked from the bed to the walls and noted that there were many sharp implements hanging on them. Before he could comment on them, he laid eyes on a masked man standing in the corner.

"Oh," Frankie said when he saw the masked man, "is he going to watch."

"Yes," the Madame said as she entered the room and closed the door behind her. "He's going to watch and he is going to *see*."

"Oh," Frankie said, still excited even though he didn't know what the Madame meant when she said "see," "I'm into it."

"Good," the Madame said as she pushed Frankie over, towards the bed. She then turned to the masked man and spoke to him. "*Snijden*," she said.

The masked man nodded one time.

Frankie jumped onto the bed and began to take his pants off.

"No, no," the Madame said. "You stand."

"Ah," Frankie said, standing, his pants around his ankles, "I see."

The Madame then removed her leather pants and crawled onto the bed. She faced him and beckoned him to come towards her.

"Please…" the Madame said, more customer-service-oriented than seductive, "enter me."

Frankie was hard before she said that. The mere act of such a dominant figure removing her bottoms and positioning herself in a vulnerable position was enough for Frankie's cock to stand as erect as it ever had been.

"Will do," Frankie said as he gripped his dick and approached her with his pants around his ankles.

If Frankie were honest, he had no idea what he was doing. He couldn't remember the last time he had been confronted with anyone who took control like this. It was pretty much new to him. He was suddenly filled with the urge to please her. He didn't want to do this woman wrong, but he didn't know what he should do when he was upon her.

"Do you want it in your ass or your pussy?" Frankie asked when his erect dick was on the precipice of entering either.

"Doesn't matter," the Madame said in broken English. "You can do with me what you wish. You are the *betalingsmaker*, no?"

"I'm whatever you need me to be, Madame," Frankie said.

He then approached the Madame and inserted himself into her vagina.

166

"I'm not going to fuck your ass yet," Frankie said as he began to pump away at her.

"You do whatever you want," the Madame said before she began to moan in the fakest pleasure that would make the best actors envious.

Frankie then began to fuck her. He gripped her by the hips and pulled her closer to him. He pulled her closer then further, then closer, again. No one's pussy (at least at that moment) had ever felt as good to him. He rammed in and out of her over and over again until he though that he couldn't take anymore.

"I'm going to move to your ass," he said, feeling as though that might relieve the orgasm he felt building up inside of him.

"Okay," the Madame said as she felt Frankie remove his cock from her cunt and place it at the precipice of her asshole.

It was all almost too much for Frankie to take. He had been given the go-ahead before, but not like that. Her adamancy had driven him to near a full on explosion of his jizz. He held it back, though. He knew he had to hold it off, at least until he knew what *snijden* was.

He pumped away at her ass. As far as he was concerned, he ravaged it. To him, his large cock was too much for her ass to handle. There was a little bit of him that knew that it could not be true, but he did not care. He just continued to fuck it. In and out, in and out. He knew that when she called out, saying that it was "too much" for her to handle, that she was laying. His horniness prevented him from hearing those words truly, however. So he just pumped and pumped away. Her ass felt too good.

"Oh yeah, oh yeah," Frankie said as he fucked her asshole. "This feels amazing."

"It feels so good," the Madame lied, then she spoke the truth. "You need to tell me when you're close."

"I'm close, baby," Frankie said as he tilted his head back. If one were watching, like the masked man, they would be remiss in thinking that he was looking to the ceiling in ecstasy. He was actually looking to the ceiling because he saw the most beautiful unicorns he had ever seen dancing above him. That image, coupled with the sensation of the Madame's ass, made Frankie feel an orgasmic feeling he hadn't felt in years.

"Oh," the Madame said, signaling to the masked man. "You're close?"

"I'm real fucking close," Frankie said as he humped away inside the Madame's ass.

As Frankie said that, the masked man grabbed one of the sharpest knives from the wall and walked up behind him. Frankie was too preoccupied to notice.

"It's coming," Frankie said before he gave one final pump. "Oh, I'm cumming, I'm cumming… Ahhhhhhh!"

Frankie spastically thrusts inside the Madame's asshole as the masked man grabbed Frankie's balls and swiftly cut them off.

It happened quicker than anyone could understand.

"Oh my fucking god," Frankie said as he seemingly came again when the deed was done. "What the fuck was that?"

Frankie then pulled out of the Madame and turned to the masked man. He saw his own testicles in the masked man's hands. His face turned the whitest it had ever been.

"What the fuck did you do?" he asked the masked man.

Before the masked man could answer, Frankie's eyes rolled back into his head. His body decided that what was transpiring, was too much to handle. He fell away from the bed onto his back.

The Madame and the masked man stared at him as he lay upon the floor.

"*Stomme Amerikaan*," the Madame said as she looked upon Frankie.

"*Ik zal hem goed maken*," the masked man said, in broken dutch, as he walked over to Frankie and began to drag him off, to a backroom.

The intention of this action (the dragging, that is) was to take Frankie to the back and stitch him up so they could "fix him".

Unbeknownst to them, even though they had both colluded in the castration of one of their patrons, nothing could ever have fixed Frankie Wood.

---

Frankie awoke in his hotel bed days later. He was lying on his stomach and he could feel the cold sting of an icepack on the place where his balls should have been. He couldn't quite remember that his testes weren't there, but something in him told him that the icepack was there for a reason.

He partially lifted himself from his sleeping position and looked around the room. He looked at the lamp that, he remembered, wouldn't shut off, before he moved his gaze to the human he acknowledged as Rachel. When he saw her, he smiled.

"Good morning, sunshine," Rachel said, smiling back.

Frankie acknowledged this greeting as a "good morning" and lifted himself up further. He was met with much discomfort as he did, so he reached around his backside to resituate the icepack. As he touched it, a clear recollection of what he had experienced came rushing back to him.

"Did I get my balls cut off?" Frankie asked.

"Yep," Rachel said matter-of-factly, with very little (if any) compassion.

"And," Miles added as he walked into the room from (what Frankie assumed was the bathroom), "it cost two-thousand dollars *Amerikaans*."

"Yep," Rachel said sarcastically, "it seems worth it."

"Fuck you," Frankie said to Rachel. "Do you know how much pain I'm in right now?"

"I can only imagine," Rachel said with all the sarcasm the world had to offer.

"You know what Rachel? You can be a real bitch sometimes," Frankie said before he turned to Miles. "So I really paid more than a grand to get my balls chopped off?"

"Well," Miles said, trying to make Frankie feel better. "You also got a wheelchair, a cane, one of those inflatable hemorrhoid pillows and a shit-ton of pain medication."

"Pain medication, you say?" Frankie asked, the thought of drugs clearly piqued his interest. "Where are the meds, then?"

Rachel sighed as she grabbed her purse. She dug around in it until she found a blank prescription bottle, full of pills of various shapes and sizes. She tossed said pill bottle to Frankie.

Frankie caught the bottle with the ease of a non-ball-less person. He eyed the bottle for a brief moment before he opened it and poured at least a fourth of the contents into his hand. He then popped those pills into his mouth and dry-swallowed them down.

It was only then that Frankie realized that Miles hadn't come from the bathroom, but from somewhere outside. Miles had two bags by his side, both seemed to be filled with booze of various varieties. Frankie motioned for Miles to give him some.

"Well you woke up like Frankie today," Miles said as he pulled a fifth of whiskey from the bag and threw it to Frankie.

"What do you mean?" Frankie asked as he caught the booze with an amazing deftness.

"You've been waking up on and off the past few days," Miles said. "And most of the time you've been non-Frankie-like. Like, we couldn't understand what you were saying."

"Yeah," Rachel agreed. "You've woken up at least three times and told us to 'write it down.' What 'it' is, we have no idea."

"Damn," Frankie said. "It must be a symptom of withdrawal. Do you guys have my other pills?"

"The shroom pills?" Rachel asked, even though she clearly knew what Frankie was talking about.

"Yes," Frankie said.

"I don't mean to sound like a broken record," Miles said, prefacing that he would, in fact, be sounding like a broken record, "but I don't think taking those pills is a good idea. Especially not now."

"Yeah, I think it'll make things worse," Rachel added.

"Thank you, Rachel," Miles said.

"Oh come on, Smiles," Frankie said as he shot a shit-eating grin to Miles and Rachel, "I think I can handle it. In fact, I think I need to handle it. I mean I know I'm ball-less, but you all should still respect me."

"We never respected you," Rachel said "with balls or without."

"Fine, Ms. Semantical," Frankie said, "I didn't mean 'respect,' I meant 'fear.' Are you happy now?"

"You're saying we should fear you?" Miles asked, semi-amused.

"If you haven't feared me by now," Frankie said. "Then you both are crazier than I must be. Now give me my actual pills or I swear to god I'll harm myself."

"More than you already have?" Rachel asked more truthfully than she intended to.

"How is that constructive?" Frankie asked. "You know I know I've hurt myself around you. I was trying to make a fucking joke."

"Well the joke isn't funny anymore, Frankie," Rachel said.

An awkward silence then took over the room. To everyone else it seemed like forever, but to Frankie it was just but a moment in time.

"Fine," Frankie eventually said, "how about I propose a trade."

"A trade for what?" Miles asked.

"Not with you," Frankie said, taking a swig from the bottle of booze, "I'm proposing a trade with Rachel. This is a Smile-less deal."

"What's the trade?" Rachel asked, forgetting the curiosity killed the cat.

"You give me *those* pills you've got," Frankie said as he held up his prescription bottle. "And I'll give you *these* pills."

"Are they worth it?" Rachel asked.

"You'll never know unless you've tried," Frankie said with a smile. It took everything in him to smile; the pain coming from where his balls used to be was almost too much to handle.

"Fine," Rachel said without much thought. "Give them here."

"You first," Frankie said, knowing that this could be one of the older tricks in the book.

Rachel sighed and threw the wooden pill container onto Frankie's bed.

"Oooh," Frankie said in a girlish squeal as he grabbed it. Once it was safely in his hands he threw his bottle to Rachel, who caught it with ease.

The two of them emptied some of the contents from their respective containers and then put said contents into their respective mouths.

"Alright," Frankie said after he felt the pills move down his throat. "So, I've got a grandmaster plan."

"What is it?" Miles asked, taking a seat on the edge of Frankie's bed.

"Is it better than the plan that involves you getting your

balls cut off and us having to push you back to the hotel in a wheelchair?" Rachel asked.

"Hey, Rachel," Frankie said, not missing the sarcasm, "we don't pay you for your thoughts. So if you're going to say shit, at least have the decency to do it with your top off."

"Oh, is that how it's going to be?" Rachel asked.

"Yep," Frankie said taking a swig of whiskey.

Rachel then tilted her head to the side with what would normally be described as a smirk (if it wasn't so wrought with chagrin). She then removed her top, unleashing her amazingly supple breasts unto the hotel room.

"Well, touché," Frankie said, "that can't be argued with. So, 'no' is the answer to your question. This idea won't involve me losing my testes again. The idea that I have is a simple one."

"Well what is it?" Rachel asked.

"Tut, tut," Frankie said, "I can't hear you unless you're fondling yourself a bit."

"Oh, like this?" Rachel said, playfully grabbing her tit in her hand and extending her long tongue down to her nipple. She couldn't quite reach, but the sentiment was enough.

"Yes, exactly," Frankie said with a smile. "Now, my idea is that we just walk around with the camera and have Rachel get naked in as many places as we possibly can."

"That seems simple enough," Miles said trying to wrap his head around the logistics. "I mean we could get some good shit with your wheelchair; it could act as a dolly."

"My thoughts exactly," Frankie said. "What do you say,

Rachel? Are you down to bring that freak to the streets?"

"I suppose I could be," Rachel said thinking about it.

"Good," Frankie said with a grin as he took more of his shroom pills, "I might need an audition, of sorts."

"Psh, what am I?" Rachel asked. "Just a construct for your male needs to get fulfilled?"

"Well," Frankie said, "I'm at least paying for you to pretend to be one."

"Well if that's what it's going to be like," Rachel said with a pout. "What did you have in mind?"

"Lose the pants," Frankie said. "Smiles, would you mind giving us the room?"

"Aw, man, c'mon," Miles said. "It's not like you can even do anything."

"I'm not doing a damn thing," Frankie said. "This is all Rachel."

"Jesus fuck," Miles said, "I don't know how to feel about this."

"You'll feel good," Frankie told him. "We've got to do something worth the plain ticket, no?"

"Well if that's what we're doing, I should be here to film it," Miles said.

"No," Frankie argued, "I'm just going to need her to work herself up. The build up needs to lead to pay off. Now, go. Let me work my magic. Don't be such a creeper, man. I thought you were better than that."

"Fine," Miles said as he grabbed a bottle of booze from his bag, "I'll be in the lobby."

"Good," Frankie said as he watched Miles leave. He then turned to Rachel. "Now lose those pants and let's see how you touch yourself when a ball-less man is watching you from across the room."

Rachel then stood up and walked over to Frankie. She took the bottle of booze from his hand and took a gulp from it.

"Hold on," Rachel said, "I need more for this."

Rachel quickly went back over to her pill bottle and grabbed a handful. She then returned to Frankie and retook the bottle. This was all before she popped the handful into her mouth and washed the pills down with the liquor.

Before Frankie could comprehend what was happening, the bottle was thrust back in his hands, and Rachel walked over to the edge of the other bed in the room. She bent over, so that her ass was facing Frankie, and removed her pants. She wasn't wearing underwear.

Rachel threw her pants at Frankie, in some sort of sick striptease, and threw herself on her back, on to the bed. She put her legs up and angled her pussy towards Frankie. Her fingers moved down her body until they reached her pussy. She used her fore- and ring fingers to spread her lips apart so that Frankie could see the beautiful, pink flesh within. Her middle finger then made its way down the center of the slit before it met the hole of herself. It slid in.

As she took it to the third knuckle, she moaned. The muscles in her hand moved and it was clear her finger was doing all the work. Her voice said "yes," and "yes," and "yes." Frankie bought the performance but, even as her toes curled, nothing ever came of it for her.

Frankie, Rachel and Miles had taken a cab to the end of the city limits. As far as they were told, they had reached the outskirts of the outskirts. When they got out of the car, Rachel and Miles looked around, unsure, before they looked back to Frankie.

"Where the fuck are we, dude?" Miles said.

"We're somewhere," Frankie said. "I had an idea."

"Well what's the idea?" Rachel asked.

"For something *big*," Frankie said. "I asked the bartender at the last spot for a place and this is where he told me to go."

"Well, it looks like we're in the middle of nowhere," Rachel said as she watched the cabdriver drive away.

"We are!" Frankie said with excitement. "But there should be a barn over there."

He then pointed off, across a large field that they were standing near. It could barely be seen in the night, but they could all just make out its white roof in the moonlight.

"You want us to go there?" Miles asked.

"Yes," Frankie said.

"And how do you purpose we do that?" Rachel asked.

"Walk," said Frankie, as though Rachel was the dumbest person he'd ever spoke to.

"Well you can't exactly walk, man," Miles said.

"Then push me, *man*, jeez," Frankie said mockingly, as he sat down in the wheelchair that they had taken out of the trunk of the cab moments ago.

"I don't know if the wheelchair can take it," Miles said.

"Well fuck it," Frankie said as he looked back to Miles. "Let's see what this baby can do."

"It's a rental," Miles said as he moved himself behind the wheel chair so he could push it.

"Fuck that," Frankie said. "They took my balls. Those aren't on lease, are they?"

"No," Miles said.

"Good, then push me towards the barn," Frankie said.

"I don't know if I can walk right," Rachel said as she stumbled where the road met the grass. "Those pills you gave me did a number on me. Not to mention the drenks."

"Drenks?" Frankie asked.

"Drinks," Rachel said clarifying, "I drank too much."

"We all drank too much and we're all not speaking rightly," Frankie said. "That's part of the fun. I want to go to the barn and see what's up. I think we can get some good shots of you, Rachel."

"I don't know…" Rachel said.

"Come on," Frankie chided. "This whole trip has to be worth something. I mean if they gave me my balls back then maybe we could sell them, but so far all we have is nada. I think if we got a nice shot of you fingering yourself in a barn, then maybe we can go home with something. Especially if we get caught. That 'getting caught' shit really sells. You know that."

"Yeah…" Rachel said, still unsure, but getting there.

"Look," Frankie said, "at least let's get there. It's right over there and we can decided once we scope it out."

"Alright…" Rachel said after some thought. "Is there no one in there? I don't want you to spring a random fuck on me."

"I won't do anything like that again," Frankie said after a laugh. "We all remember what happened last time. All I want to do is have a little bit of an adventure and shoot *something* so we don't go back empty-handed."

"Okay," Rachel said, "I think I can make it there."

"We can all make it there," Frankie said before he turned to Miles who was standing over his shoulder; ready to push the wheelchair, "as long as Smiles makes it like a rollercoaster."

"What about your ball-less ass?" Miles asks.

"Can't feel a thing," Frankie said. "Thanks to shrooms and booze."

"Well I'll see what I can do," Miles said.

"You want a ride?" Frankie asked Rachel.

"That would help," Rachel responded.

Rachel walked over and sat on Frankie's lap in the wheelchair. Frankie made a gesture to move forward and Miles pushed them in the wheelchair across the field. They went at great speed and laughed all the while. Frankie put his hands up so as to enjoy the experience more. Every bump they hit made them feel as though they were about to lose control, but every "jump" they landed made them experience life more.

Soon they were at the barn. They found, when they were there, that it was a stable.

"Oh what the fuck?" Rachel asked when she saw it. "You know this shit doesn't sell. Are you really trying to get me to do bestiality?"

"No, no, no," Frankie said, trying to act offended. "Well, not really. I mean, I don't want you to fuck any of these *beasts*, but just get up close to them naked. The bartender-guy said they were docile."

"Oh my god, Frankie, no!" Rachel said before she stormed off.

"Where is she going?" Frankie asked, acting offended.

"Back the way we came," Miles said, watching after her.

"Well fuck," Frankie said, "I'm starting to doubt her commitment to this. I mean, I lost my balls. What more does she need?"

"She's just drunk," Miles said, stumbling slightly from the drinks he, himself, had drank. "Maybe I should go check on her?"

"Yeah, man," Frankie said. "Talk her into what I'm seeing. You know what I'm seeing right? Nothing *uncouth*, I just want to make something grand."

"I get it, man," Miles said as he went to walk off.

"Hey, wait," Frankie said, before Miles could get too far away. "Give me the camera so I can set up."

"Alright," Miles said as he went to his backpack and produced a camcorder. He handed it to Frankie, "Here you go."

Frankie took the camera and lined up the shot as best he could. He focused on a horse that was standing in front of him behind a gate. He zoomed the camera in and out on its face.

"Who's a good horse?" Frankie asked to no real avail. "Yes, you are."

The horse let out what Frankie had assumed was a neigh, but was some other horse-noise, altogether.

"God damn," Frankie said when he heard it. "This is going to be good."

"My god," Frankie heard Rachel say as he looked through the viewfinder, "I can't believe I'm drunk enough to let *Miles* talk me into this shit."

"Eh," Frankie said with little sympathy, "we've all been there."

"Hey now!" Miles said as he escorted Rachel into the shot Frankie had set up. "I'm offended."

"There's no time for that," Frankie said. "Are you down to do this, Rachel?"

"Yes," Rachel said as though she'd been asked this question a million times. "What do you want me do to?"

"Well," Frankie said with a smile, as he went back to the camcorder to line up a shot. "Let's start by having you take off your clothes."

"*Clothes*," Rachel said with a laugh as she pulled off her sundress (she had changed before they left the hotel), "I'd hardly call this shit '*clothes*.'"

"Well semantics aside," Frankie said as he looked through the viewfinder, "you look great."

"Oh really?" Rachel asked sarcastically. "Thank you so much, Frankie Wood, for telling me what I already knew. *Jesus Fuck*."

"There's no need to be that way," Frankie said, lining things up. "You look good right there- wait, no -Is there any way I can get you to go into the pen with it?"

"Wait what?" Rachel asked, she laid the drunken sass

on thick. "You want me to go in there with that thing?"

"Yeah," Frankie said, "I'm not asking you to, like, fuck it or anything. I just want to see you next to it. The shot calls for it." Frankie then motioned to the camera he was looking through.

"Alright," Rachel said as she turned to Miles, "if shit goes wrong you get me the fuck out of there okay?"

"Okay," Miles said, unsure if he could do what was being asked of him.

"Okay," Rachel repeated with a nod before she opened the gate and entered the horse's stall.

"That looks good," Frankie said. "Can you jump around a bit?"

"What? Ugh, fine," Rachel said with a sigh before she put a shit-eating grin on her face and began to jump around in a way that she had found made men aroused. "Is that good?" She asked mid-jump.

"Looks great," Frankie said, looking through the camera. "Is there a way you can get close to it?"

The horse had awoken when Rachel had begun to jump around. It made both her and Miles slightly anxious. Frankie had ignored it.

"Are you sure it's okay?" Miles asked.

"It's fine," Frankie said to Miles, before he spoke to Rachel. "Move closer, will you?"

"I don't know, Frankie," Rachel said, eyeing the horse who was clearly showing signs that it didn't want to be messing around with humans at that moment.

"Just get in there, Rachel," Frankie said. "It's not going to hurt you. It's more afraid of you than you are of it."

182

"I don't-" Rachel tried to say.

"Rachel!" Frankie shouted, making the horse more uneasy. "I'm looking into this camera right now, and I'm telling you that what I'm seeing isn't what we need. You've got to get closer to that fucking thing. It ain't going to bite you."

"Alright, alright," Rachel said, offended. "There's no need to use that tone."

Frankie watched in the viewfinder as Rachel inched closer and closer to the unsure animal.

"Pet it, Rachel," Frankie said as he watched on. "It looks uneasy. Try to calm it down."

"Well of cou-" Rachel tried to say before Frankie cut her off.

"Don't get uppity," Frankie said. "You're going to scare it more. Just pet the fucking thing."

"Oh hey, horsey," Rachel said as she placed her hand upon its mane. "How are you? You're a good horsey, yeah?"

The horse neighed.

"Great!" Frankie said. "That takes care of formalities. How about you move down south."

"What?" Rachel asked, pretending she'd misheard.

"Move closer to its dick, Rachel," Frankie said as though she was the dumbest thing he'd ever spoken to.

"I don't-" Rachel tried to say. Again, Frankie cut her off.

"I'm not asking you to fuck the thing," Frankie said. "It's just that when you're close to his head it steals focus. I'm looking right at the shot, Rachel."

"Okay, okay," Rachel said as she slowly moved away from the horse's head, passed its flank, towards its buttocks.

"You think we can call this one 'Black Pubey?'" Frankie asked Miles. "Or will people not get the reference?"

"I think that might be kind of a stretch," Miles said, eyeing the brown horse that the naked Rachel stood in front of.

"Yeah, but-" Frankie tried to say before Rachel butt in.

"I'm at his ass, Frankie," Rachel said. "Can I get out of here now?"

"Rub his ass a bit," Frankie said, looking through the camera. "Like pet it."

She did as she was told and patted the horse on his butt.

"Moan a bit," Frankie said, "I think the viewers want to see that you're enjoying this."

Rachel moaned as she rubbed the horse's buttocks. She went to play with its tail, but the horse seemed to not like that.

"Is that good?" She asked, after she'd clearly had enough.

"I don't know," Frankie said. "We're going for soft-core bestiality here and all this fucking horse is giving me is 'nude girl standing near a horse.' Could you maybe entice him a bit?"

"What?" Rachel asked, who even in her drunken state had hoped that she misheard.

"Could you just maybe touch his dick?" Frankie asked.

"I'm not saying you have to fuck it, but like, since you're there, could you like just tap it? I mean, just to let him know everything is okay?"

"Is that how horses know things are okay?" Rachel said, unsure.

"Yeah, of course," Frankie said, cocksure as ever. "Everyone knows that the easiest way to calm a horse down is to grab it by the dick. Right, Smiles?"

"Um, sure," Miles said, clearly not a fan of what was transpiring, but willing to be a participant just the same.

"See?" Frankie said. "Miles knows what's up. Just touch his dick- maybe stroke it a little -and everything will be okay."

"If you guys say so," Rachel said as she brought her hand up, across the horse's back around its hip, across its thigh and down towards the stifle, where, she assumed, its dick was. She moved her hand around there as she tried to shush the horse whenever it attempted to have an uproar. It seemed to listen to her for at least awhile.

"Yes, like that," Frankie said as he watched her hands move around the horse through the camcorder.

"Where's its cock at?" Rachel said as she felt around the horse's underside.

"It should be right-" Frankie tried to say before the horse reared up.

"Oh fuck," Rachel said as the horse violently moved around its enclosure.

"Wait," Frankie said as he watched it happen through the viewfinder, "is that a girl horse?"

"No!" Miles shouted as he watched Rachel struggle.

"Get the fuck out of there, Rachel!"

But his calls were too late; the horse had already kicked its back legs.

The horse's hock came back towards Rachel as it kicked and she was hit with the full force of its leg returning. She didn't see it coming, for she was dodging the initial kick. The blow of the horse's cannon bone was enough to knock her to the floor.

Once she was on the floor, nothing could be done for her.

"Oh my god," Frankie said as he watched through the camera.

"Fuck, fuck, fuck," Miles said as he watched the horse trample Rachel into the floor.

Her brain-matter and the hay the horse had been shitting in became one. All that could be seen was a woman's limp body and a shitty, brown mess.

"Oh my god," Miles said.

"Well this didn't go as expected," Frankie said as he took his eye away from the camera and saw what was actually unfolding in front of him.

"Is…" Miles said, obviously in shock, "Is she okay?"

"We have to get the fuck out of here," Frankie said as he turned to Miles.

All Miles could focus on was the body in the horse pen. Frankie slapped him.

"Fucking, get with it!" Frankie shouted, "We've got to get out of here!"

Miles didn't move, he kept staring, clearly in shock. Frankie slapped him again.

"If we don't leave soon," Frankie said, "we're going to be fucked!"

Miles didn't want to be fucked, and so he grabbed Frankie's wheelchair and pushed him towards the road. He knew they'd call a cab eventually when they got there. If they got there. Wherever there was. Miles really couldn't see where he was going from under the tears.

---

The initial thought was that they should leave Amsterdam immediately. Although, once Frankie had realized he needed to sleep and had read the next-day's paper he knew that they could stay for as long as they pleased. There was no mention of Rachel in the paper Frankie read when he awoke the next morning. Nor the morning after that, nor the morning after that, even.

No one had seemed to care about Rachel's death in Amsterdam, save for Miles, who, even days after, couldn't seem to shut up about it.

"I can't believe we left her there…" Miles said, after he'd had at least a fifth of some vodka to himself.

"We're all bummed about it," Frankie reassured. "I mean I can't believe I didn't hit the record button. Who would've thought that I'd fuck up that big?"

"*You* fucked up that big?" Miles said. "Fuck, you know Rachel's dead right? I mean she's dead. She's gone. Goner than gone. She got stomped into nothing, and you're thinking about not hitting fucking record, man, seriously?"

"Yeah," Frankie said, popping shroom pills into his

mouth, "I mean, don't get me wrong, it's shitty, but that shit could have been huge. Do you even know how much an actual snuff film could go for? Much less one with bestiality. We could have sold to the highest bidder, and that bidder would have probably paid at least seven figures outright. It could have been brilliant. Beyond brilliant! I don't even know if there's a word for it!"

Frankie laughed as he took even more pills and looked up, to the ceiling. The ceiling looked back at him and smiled and nodded. To Frankie that was a sign of reassurance.

"See?" Frankie said, thinking Miles saw the ceiling as well. "We know what's up. You could know what's up too if you'd be willing to meet me halfway. Maybe then you wouldn't be such a sad-sack."

"Sad-sack?" Miles said with as much of a laugh as he'd been to muster since he witnessed Rachel's death. "You think me dealing with this makes me a sad-sack? For real? I think those pills are making you insane."

"Déjà-fucking-vu," Frankie said with a laugh as he popped even more pills into his mouth. "We've heard this song before."

"I don't give a fu-" Miles began to say.

"Shhh!" Frankie said as he held his hand up. He wore a look on his face that expressed that he might have come up with the best idea he'd ever had.

"What is it?" Miles asked, clearly done with Frankie and his seemingly insurmountable pile of bullshit.

"I think…" Frankie said, not being able to find the reassurance he needed until he looked up to the ceiling, which told him to go on, "I think I've just had my best idea yet."

Frankie then did that thing that most people do; he let the thought hang there like bait. He wanted Miles to pry. He wanted to feel like the thought he had was so important that it couldn't just be said. To him, it was *that* important. Miles could not care less.

"Ugh," Frankie said after Miles didn't ask what he was talking about. "Do you want to hear it or not?"

"Honestly?" Miles asked, putting his head in his hands.

"Yes, mother-fucker," Frankie said, "I'm not going to say it if it's going to fall on deaf ears."

"Well then don't say it," Miles said. "I'm done with this shit. I can't handle any more of your ideas."

"What the fuck is wrong with you, Smiles?" Frankie asked, offended.

"What's wrong with me?!" Miles yelled. "What's fucking wrong with me?!" he repeated, near exacerbation. "Are you fucking kidding me? Like do you even hear yourself? No, not even that- Fuck! Do you even hear me? Did you even hear Rachel? I mean, fuck, dude, you've lost your fucking mind."

"What the fuck are you even talking about?" Frankie asked, matching Miles' anger. "I listen. I listen all the time. And all I'm hearing is fucking nothing. Zero. Zilch. Nada. I talk and talk and talk and all I get back is fucking a grand abyss of stupidity. No one listens to me. You think it's my fault Rachel's dead? Fuck, if she would have listened to me, the video would have been great. It really would have. But she wanted nothing to do with it. She was scared and that poor animal is now a murderer because of it. Thank god it was a dumbass horse, 'cause if it was something with any thought in its dumbass head then it would be haunted by guilt for the rest of its dumbass life."

"*It* would be haunted?" Miles asked. "Are you fucking with me? *It*? It shouldn't be haunted, *you* should be haunted you dumb mother-fucker. I-"

"Hey!" Frankie shouted. "Don't you call me a 'mother-fucker', I ain't no mother-fucker."

"Well you're definitely a piece-of-shit," Miles said. "You can't deny that. You don't even give a shit. Why are you pretending you care?"

"Because it's what you humans do," Frankie said, chuckling. "Haven't you gotten it yet? I'm a fucking god to you. I am Rah. I am Zeus. Not the ones you know but the ones you will know."

"You think you're a god?" Miles asked, he couldn't even laugh. "For real? You fucking egotistical prick. You direct shitty porno, you fuck. You aren't shit. You might even be worse than it."

"Exactly, man," Frankie said, popping more pills. "Fucking exactly. I agree with you one hundred percent. But I swear to fucking god I'm worth more than that. All I am now is a fucking nobody porn director. I could be great, though. That's all I ever wanted. That's all I've ever strived for. I want to be *the* porn director. I want to make the greatest porno ever made. I want people to die when they cum. I want the life of them to sprawl out of them into the napkin or towel or toilet paper or toilet bowl or keyboard or fucking whatever. I want them only to be able to jack off to my stuff."

"That won't happen," Miles said. "You have to have figured that out by now."

"Fuck you," Frankie said. "That's too one-dimensional. That's just fucking dumb. I know that it *shouldn't* happen, but I still believe it *could*. And that's what I'm striving for. If I give up on my dreams, I'm done man. All of this is done. And you don't think that gets to me? You don't think the heft of having to worry about you and Maxine's success gets to me? I mean fuck, if we keep making the shit we've been making, we're done. Then what? What do you guys do for work after you've got a large gap in your employment history? I mean, you can't tell future employers you spent a fucking decade making porn. And do you really think you'll get anywhere in the industry without me?"

"I don't know, man," Miles said. "I don't care anymore."

"Well you should care," Frankie said. "It's your fucking future."

"My future is fucked, Frankie," Miles said, "I watched one of my best friends get stomped to fucking death by a horse. And so did you. You should care, but you don't. I can't wrap my mind around that."

"You can't wrap your mind around much," Frankie said.

"Dude," Miles said, "your insults mean very little to me right now. I don't care about any of that. I just want to know what we're supposed to do next. Where the fuck do you go once you've just stood by as you watch someone you love get killed?"

"You go up," Frankie said, matter-of-factly. "You've got no-where to go but up. If you think about the bullshit we've seen for too long, you'll stay down and move down and down and down and down. All we can do is take what we've seen and use it to help us."

"How does this help us?" Miles asked, looking into Frankie's eyes. "Please, tell me how this helps us."

"Well," Frankie said, "for one, it helps us grow desensitized."

"Desensitized? To what?" Miles asked.

"For the thing that will make us goddamn legends," Frankie said.

"Are you saying what I think you're saying?" Miles asked.

"What do you think I'm saying?" Frankie asked in return.

"I need to hear you say it," Miles said.

"Oh," Frankie said with a laugh, "now you want to hear it."

"Screw you," Miles said. "Just fucking say what you want to do. I need to know you're the full-blown psychopath I've watched you grow into."

"I haven't grown into anything," Frankie said. "I've always been this way."

Miles didn't know what to say to that.

Frankie looked at Miles smugly, as he popped more shroom pills into his mouth. He then rolled over to lay on his back, in the bed, and stared back at the ceiling. It was now scowling at him. The ceiling opened its mouth and flames shot from it. The fire didn't touch Frankie, though. He knew it wouldn't. So he kept the smug look on his face as he put his hands behind his head and closed his eyes.

"So, what?" Miles asked, after a long bit of silence. "You aren't going to tell me now?"

"Do you really want to know?" Frankie said, not opening his eyes.

"Not really," Miles said. "But if you don't tell me, who else are you going to tell?"

Frankie sighed. He knew Miles was right. He knew he needed to tell someone. Miles wasn't acting worthy, however, so it irked Frankie that this was to be his audience. He rolled the alternatives through his head, but there was no one better than Miles. Frankie knew that he had to say it, he didn't want to, but he knew he had to. He sighed again when the realization hit him.

"Alright," Frankie said, "but I don't want you to freak out."

"I'll do what I need to," Miles said. "Just fucking say it."

"Fine, here it is," Frankie then rolled over onto his side and looked Miles in the eyes. "I want to make a snuff film."

"Oh fuck off," Miles said. "No-fucking-way. I'm not going to cast that shit, I'm not going to be apart of it."

"You don't have to cast anyone," Frankie said. "I know who we'll use."

"Who?" Miles said before he realized it, the realization

hit his face before it left his mouth. "Maxine?"

Frankie didn't say anything; he smirked and rolled over onto his back.

"No," Miles said, sounding a bit like a broken record. "No, no, no. Absolutely not. No fucking way!"

"Why not?" Frankie said. "Why fucking not? It's not like she has to know. I mean Rachel didn't know. We can just stage it like Rachel's thing."

"*Rachel's* thing?" Miles said, standing. "You fucking lunatic. You killed Rachel and now you want to kill Maxine!"

"A horse killed Rachel," Frankie said.

"No, Frankie," Miles said. "*We* killed Rachel. You and fucking me. You told her what to do, I knew it was a bad idea, I did nothing. I talked her into it. We fucked up. We fucked up bad and now you want to repeat that fuck-up? Wasn't one death enough for you?"

"Sure, if I filmed it," Frankie said, thinking that Miles' question was not rhetorical. "But I didn't. Look, Miles, we're on the edge of creating art here and-"

"Porn isn't art!" Miles yelled, pointing his finger at Frankie. "And you're goddamn crazy!"

"Crazy makes the world go 'round," Frankie said, as he closed his eyes again and put his arms behind his head.

"No!" Miles said, approaching Frankie. "Fuck you, you insane fuck! You insane, selfish fuck! You walk all over everyone you fucking know and now you want to- what? - be a serial killer? How many people do you have to kill? Fuck! Fuck man! God damn it! She's gone! She's fucking gone. And what are we going to do about that?

194

What the fuck are we going to do?! How are we going to tell people what we did? Have you thought about what we're going to tell James?"

"Ha!" Frankie said, not opening his eyes. "Maybe once he experiences some fucking pain he'll be able to write something worth filming."

"You are such a..." Miles couldn't think of how to finish his statement. What else could be really said? He let his shoulders fall and the anger seemed to leave him. Perhaps it turned into something else.

"Aw," Frankie said sarcastically, "be careful or you might hurt my feelings."

"We're leaving tomorrow," Miles said and then he walked into the bathroom of the hotel room and slammed the door. Frankie could hear the shower turn on.

"Oh come on," Frankie said, opening his eyes and sitting up as best he could. "Look, Miles, don't stress out about it! I'll send James an email from Rachel saying that she just wants to stay here. I mean, fuck man, maybe he'll come looking for her. Then we'd kill two birds," he waited for the joke to land, but all he heard was the sound of the water running. "I guess it doesn't matter since I can fire him when Maxine's gone," he then said to himself.

Frankie then fell back onto the pillow on the bed and looked back to the ceiling. The face he had been seeing was gone. Frankie couldn't help but feel like it had abandoned him. Just like Miles. Everyone seemed, to Frankie, to abandon him. That's when he felt the loneliest that he'd ever felt.

"Miles!" Frankie yelled at the top of his lung. "Fucking

Miles! C'mon! Smiles! Smiles! SMILES!"

There was no response to this, however. Just the shower. It droned on and on and on. It drove Frankie nearly crazy to hear it. It became a noise that took over all of his senses. His ears couldn't hear anything else; his nose could smell the water. When he closed his eyes all he could see was a grand waterfall pouring down and down and down. He could feel the water it was generating began to cover him. It started at his toes and moved up his ankles. Soon, in his mind, it had passed his missing balls and was moving up his chest. He couldn't help but feel that he was submerged. He knew, then, that Miles was trying to drown him.

He opened his eyes abruptly and saw that Miles wasn't filling the room with water. Miles was still in the bathroom, letting the shower run. Despite the jolt of reality, Frankie couldn't help but still think that Miles was out to get him. He knew in his heart of hearts that it was Miles' goal. Perhaps it had been his goal all along.

Frankie then decided that Miles needed to be stopped. He knew, though, that he couldn't risk doing it in Amsterdam. It had to wait until he was home. If he didn't take care of it quickly, Miles would surely ruin him, in one way or another.

"I'll show you a serial killer," Frankie then said under his breath, even though he knew no one could hear him. He then closed his eyes and sleep overtook him shortly thereafter.

# THE FINAL ACT OF
# THE GREATEST PORNO EVER MADE

His name was Frankie Wood and he was leading one of the actors in his masterpiece up to his room. He was unbelievably high on shroom pills and the world around him was vibrant and alive with possibilities. Despite the fact that he was hobbling on a cane, there was an undeniable pep to his step. He was too excited for what was to come to be able to contain it.

James, the actor Frankie was leading up the stairs, could see it. Frankie's excitement made James excited. He wanted to be apart of something that could make the normally pessimistic person as optimistic as Frankie seemed. By the time Frankie led James into his room and shut the door behind him, he could hardly hold in the positive energy he was feeling. It was the best James had felt since Rachel told him she wouldn't be returning from Amsterdam.

"So, what's this twist, man?" James asked as Frankie led him to the middle of the room. James rubbed his hands together, letting his anticipation be shown. Frankie could also see a promising look in James' eyes.

"Look, James," Frankie said, "I've got to come clean with you…"

"Alright, Frankie. What's up?" James asked, not apprehensive in the slightest.

"Well," Frankie said, "it's just that I don't like you very much. I used to. For some reason I don't now. Why do you think that is? Do you think we've grown apart?"

"I always assumed it was because me and Rachel got together," James said, without batting an eye. "I just figured it got in the way of whatever you were trying to do with her."

"You're a fool if you think Rachel and I still didn't keep on keepin' on after she started fucking you," Frankie said. "I mean, no offense, but you had nothing on me. She liked to be bit, you don't like to bite. You think she'd stick around with you just 'cause you guys made sweet, sweet love?"

"Come on, man," James said. "Why do you have to be like this?"

"I am what I am," Frankie said.

"Look, man," James said, "I didn't come up here to have you shit all over me, okay? You know I'm missing Rachel, there's no need to get all *Frankie* about it."

"I can't not get '*Frankie*' about it," Frankie said. "I think you should get over Rachel. She's a dumb cunt and she ain't coming back."

"Whatever, man," James said, "I don't need this shit right now."

James went to leave, but Frankie grabbed him by the shoulder.

"If you walk out of here, James," Frankie said, looking the large, black man before him square in the eyes. "You better not ever come back. I'm not kidding. I don't know what will happen to you."

"Is that a threat?" James said.

"No," Frankie said, "it's absolutely the opposite."

James then looked at Frankie, clearly confused. It's then he really saw Frankie for the first time since he'd been back from Amsterdam. Frankie's eyes were sunken and wild. His blonde hair was matted and greasy. His skin looked drier than dry. It seemed as though it could flake off at anytime. There was something pathetic about Frankie in that moment, and James couldn't help but feel something for the man that used to be his friend.

"Are you okay, Frankie?" James asked. "I'm worried about you; you don't look so good."

"No," Frankie said almost too-dramatically as he let go of James' shoulder, "I'm not doing well at all."

Frankie then hobbled over to his messy, cluttered desk, and sat down, rather uncomfortably, on his wobbly chair. He tried to do it in the most sympathetic manner. It turned out that this was the best way to go.

"Well, what is it, man?" James said. "You've been a real dick lately. I mean no offense, but you aren't the same Frankie I met. You haven't been in awhile."

"I don't know, man," Frankie said. "I've just been caught up with this idea lately, even before Amsterdam. But going there opened it up in my mind. It made it more ferocious. Now this idea just fucking continues to claw at me and, quite honestly, it's driving me nuts. I almost can't take it. It's turning me into an asshole (I know that), and I apologize for it."

"Frankie, man, you don't have to apologize for shit as long as you feel sorry," James said with a friendly smile. "I know you're always going through shit. I just want you to know that I'm here for you."

"Thanks, man, I appreciate it," Frankie said. "I know I don't deserve it."

"Don't sweat it," James said. "Just let me know if there's anything I can do for you."

"Well," Frankie said, looking up like a child trying to get something. "You could help me with my masterpiece."

"I would love to," James said. "I really would."

"You said you were going to leave, though," Frankie said with a little bit of a pout that James could not see through.

"I won't, man," James said. "I won't."

"You promise?" Frankie said.

"Yeah, for sure," James said walking over to Frankie, "I've got you. Tell me what you want to do."

"Don't you already know what I want to do?" Frankie said. "I want to shoot this great thing with Maxine."

"Well yeah," James said. "But you'd said you had some sort of twist you wanted to tell me."

"Oh yeah!" Frankie said, standing up in remembrance. "I almost forgot about the twist."

"Well lay it on me, man," James said.

"Can I trust you, though?" Frankie asked. "I mean, are

you sure you don't want to just walk away?"

"I'm not going to walk away," James said. "I was just getting all sore because of you lashing out."

"You promise?" Frankie asked, again, grabbing James by the shoulder (this time in a non-threatening way).

"I promise," James said, genuinely.

"Alright," Frankie said, "I gave you a way out."

"Ha!" James laughed, thinking Frankie was joking, "Man, you always give me a way out. Just tell me what this twist is so we can shoot this awesome thing you've got planned."

"Well, James," Frankie began, gripping the head of his cane. "I've got to tell you, the twist is, at least to you, that you aren't going to be in this picture."

"What?" James asked, genuinely confused. "Then why did you make such a big deal out of all of this?"

"Ummm…" Frankie said, trying to think of something to say, but coming up with nothing.

Instead of saying anything Frankie whipped his cane around and hit James in the side of the head. It wasn't enough force to knock James on his ass, but James was clearly dazed.

James looked at Frankie, as though he was saying, "What the fuck?" with his eyes. He opened his mouth, perhaps to say what his eyes were trying to communicate, but before anything could escape his lips he was met with another blow by Frankie's cane.

That blow made him fall to the floor.

Frankie then stood over him and lifted the cane above his head. James opened his eyes and saw, through the tunnel vision that was setting in, Frankie bring the cane down. James closed his eyes as he felt the cane hit his forehead. There was a loud CRACK and James could feel a warm liquid spurt into his closed eyes as a ringing filled his ears.

Frankie lifted the cane again and brought it down, that time with much more force. The crack that the cane-upon-skull made this time was far louder than the first one. Frankie did it again and again, though, and soon the cracks turned into thuds and the thuds turned into a sound that would be sickening to anyone who wasn't deranged; it was a warm, soft squishing noise.

To Frankie, James' skull had turned into two. At least almost. James' head had almost been split in two by the sheer blunt-force of the cane. The top of his cranium, coupled with the copious amounts of blood, had almost made James look as though he were the devil.

"Noh-Fra" James said, in a gurgle as he put his hands up and grabbed the cane during what would have been the penultimate blow. His hands gripped the slick cane and held on, the adrenaline in him was clearly giving him nearly super-human strength.

Unfortunately, Frankie believed he too had super-human strength. Perhaps it was the shroom pills or perhaps it was just who he had become. Either way, Frankie lifted his foot up and brought it down on James' face. There was a large crunch. The crunch was a sound that broke the world. Frankie was too high to notice, though.

Frankie then was able to wiggle the cane from James'

grasp. He watched as James' hands fell to the floor.

For a moment, Frankie thought his deed was done, but he figured he better be on the safe side. He brought the cane back up and down, over and over and over again, until the palms of his hands ached with the reverberations of the cane hitting the floor.

Frankie then repositioned how he carried the cane. He choked up on it and then brought it down, as though he was using it to stab, and jammed the head of the cane into what used to be James' face.

He did that repeatedly until he could feel the floor. At some point, he must have closed his eyes, because when he opened them he looked down and saw that James was nothing but a body. His head was a puddle. Less than a puddle, even, just merely a spurt, a trickle. If Frankie had taken a picture of James, it might have looked as though James' head exploded.

It took Frankie awhile to catch his breath. His head was spinning like crazy. He couldn't help but think about how out-of-shape he must be. He fell to his knees, straddling (what used to be) James. His breath was heavy, his hands ached. He let the cane fall to the side as he stared at where James' eyes used to be.

"Fuck you," Frankie said to him. "You cliché fuck."

He punched the muck, but only hit the floor. It hurt his hand and he let out a cry of pain.

As he rubbed his hurt hand he heard a knock on the door. He froze as he heard it and turned to the door with wide eyes.

Before Frankie could move, the door began to open.

"Hey Frankie," Tony said as he opened the door. "Maxine is pretty far gone I think we should probably get this show on the-"

Once Tony had fully entered the room, he looked around and saw the following tableau:

Frankie, splattered in blood, was sitting atop a body. The face of the body was so disfigured (if not 'nonexistent') that it took Tony a moment to realize that the body must have been James. A bloody cane was sitting there, bloodier than Frankie.

"What the fuck?" Tony asked, without really thinking about it.

"God damn it, Tony," Frankie said.

Frankie went to move towards Tony. Before Frankie could reach him, Tony lunged for the cane. He wheeled it around and hit Frankie in the back.

Instead of hurting Frankie, it seemed to just make him angrier. He turned to Tony and pushed the cane away with his forearm. As the cane flew from Tony's hand, Frankie wrapped his hands around Tony's throat.

Frankie gripped his throat with everything he could muster. That force proved to be too much for Tony to handle. It made Tony make a horrible gurgling noise.

Soon, Tony's eyes rolled back inside his head and Frankie clenched his teeth as he squeezed and squeezed and squeezed. Before Frankie knew it, Tony went completely limp. Frankie let go and watched as Tony fell to the floor

Once that happened, a strange feeling washed over Frankie. It took him a moment to realize that this feeling was, in fact, sobriety. He hadn't taken his pills in some time, and now he was forced to confront reality.

The reality he was confronting was that he was standing over Tony's body, mere feet from a faceless (even headless) James. Both weren't moving. It appeared as though the only living soul in Frankie's room was Frankie himself.

That was until Frankie heard a desperate breath escape Tony's lips.

Frankie looked down at Tony, noting full well that he was still alive. Sobriety was coming quick, and Frankie didn't know what to do.

He stood over Tony, who was clearly unconscious and struggling for breath.

"Die, you fuck," Frankie whispered as he looked down at Tony.

Tony didn't die, though. He gasped and gasped in slumber. Frankie shook his head at that.

"Jesus fuck," Frankie said. "You can't do anything right."

Frankie then patted down his own pockets and found his little wooden pill container. He took more than a few out and dry-swallowed them down. A sigh left his mouth after he'd done it, and he shook off the mild pain he had in his throat. It was no match for the pain his hands felt, but that pain was just a strange burning. Surely, they ached, yet still they yearned for more. Frankie looked at them for a moment before he fully realized what he must do.

He knelt down near Tony, reached over and grabbed his cane (which was a few feet away) and gripped it with both hands, one hand near the base, the other near the top. He put the shaft of his cane, the part between his two hands, against Tony's throat.

Frankie then held it there, applying more and more pressure, putting the whole of his body's weight onto it. Tony's unconscious body struggled, but Frankie persisted. It took nearly fifteen minutes before all the life had left Tony's body.

---

Maxine had taken pill after pill. She had been told, by Frankie, that her body should be numb to her. It took her awhile to get there and while she was getting there, she had, perhaps, taken too many of those pills. Her body was numb and then some. It tingled and was heavy. She tried to lift her arm to look at her hands, but it was of no use. It was too much effort.

Around the time she realized her body was all but useless, she heard the door to the garage/studio open.

"Hello?" she asked, although in her current state it sounded more like "huhoh."

"It's just me, Maxine," Frankie said before she could see him.

She tried to lift her head to look at where Frankie was but her body couldn't be bothered. However, she could hear Frankie's footstep (along with the drop of a cane) as he walked over to one of the cameras. She then heard the sound of a record-button being pressed before she heard Frankie coming over to her. Frankie's body could be felt sitting near the end of the bed.

"How're you doing, Maxine?" Frankie asked, his voice was strange. Maxine could not place what was wrong with it.

"I'm okay," Maxine said, forcing herself to really enunciate. "I can't feel my legs or my hands or my legs."

"Damn," Frankie said with a chuckle. "You must have taken a lot of relaxers, yeah?"

"Yep," Maxine said. She meant to nod as she said it, but such a gesture was impossible for her body to perform.

"Well I guess I should catch up," Frankie said. Maxine could then hear Frankie's little pill container be opened and then the sound of Frankie swallowing.

"Too many pills," was all Maxine could say. She meant to say that Frankie was, maybe, taking too many pills, but all that came out was "Too many pills."

"Yeah," Frankie seemed to agree. "We'll need a lot of pills to get through this."

Maxine then felt a strange sensation upon the skin of her legs. It took her a moment to realized that the tingling must be the feeling of Frankie moving his finger down her leg, from her thigh, all the way to her feet. He moved his finger between her toes. It felt strange, it almost hurt; it was oddly cold and felt wet, perhaps.

"God," Frankie exclaimed, "I have always loved your feet."

Before Maxine could say anything, she felt Frankie scoot up from the base of the bed towards her head. Frankie's face entered her eyesight. He looked down at her. There was a sadness in his eyes, something she had seen a million times before, but never with this depth. It seemed as though his sorrow was burrowed deep inside of him and was trying to wave to her, through his large, black eyes, letting her know that it was there.

"What is it?" Maxine asked.

"What do you mean, my dear?" Frankie asked, in return.

"You... Sad..." were the only words that Maxine's mouth could form from her thoughts.

"I am sad, Maxine," Frankie said as his finger moved up to her face. Again, even though she couldn't see it, it felt as though his finger was hurting her in some way.

"Why?" Maxine asked. All she wanted to do was close her eyes, but she also really wanted to know why Frankie, a man she loved, seemed to be in so much pain.

"I'm going to kill you Maxine..." Frankie said as she saw his eyes staring straight into hers. "I'm going to do it because I love you. I'm going to kill you because I can't have you. It's not your fault I can't have you. It's mine. But I can't live with it and this is the only option I can see. I'm sorry, but I hope you understand."

"No..." Maxine said, the realization of what was happening hit her drug-succumbed mind. Even in the stupor she found herself in, the heft of Frankie's words could still be understood. Her brain tried to tell her body to move, but her body would not listen. Her body was somewhere else.

"Yes, Maxine, yes," Frankie said. "Don't you see what you've done to me? I mean you have to have seen it. You're a smart girl. Don't you see that you've made me this way? I can't look at myself in the mirror anymore. I haven't been able to in years. Every time I do I see this gross, disgusting mass. It's the mass you left. The mass you abandoned. Just a lump of shit you thought you could do without. For years I thought it was me. For years and years! And sure, I guess when you boil it down, it was all me, but one thing that no one ever thinks about is that their opinions of other people, even if they're only perceived, can be so fucking detrimental. You see, Maxine, you're fucking opinion of me, at least the one I think you have (because you've never told me otherwise) is what I saw myself as. You clearly saw me as a piece-of-shit and so, I, obliviously, began to see myself in the same light. So, really, how is this all not your fault? How are you not the one who deserves punishment for unleashing *Frankie Fucking Wood* onto the world? Don't you see what you've done to me? Fuck! Don't you see it? Just look at me! Fucking look at me, Maxine!"

Maxine could feel Frankie's firm grip on her face as he turned her gaze towards him. She had tried to look away, but he clearly wouldn't let her.

"You see, Maxine? Do you see?" Frankie said with a wild look in his eyes. "I can't be a normal human being anymore. That only gives me two options. There's just two fucking things that I can do. And really, when you think about it *rationally*, you'll see that there's only one. There is only one thing to do. I have to kill you Maxine. I fucking have to. I have to because it will teach you a lesson. I hope there's an afterlife that you'll be able to lament this in, I really hope there is, but if not, I'll still imagine it. My imagination has always gotten the best of me. Of us. Of all of us. Every last one of us fell victim to it. And that's another reason you must die. You have to die so that I do it and I realize that I am an actual monster. You see, I sit here thinking about it. I'm like, '*No, Frankie, you can't be a monster*,' but I know it deep, deep down that I am. I just have to prove that to myself. I suppose that's the real reason that I have to do this. I've done everything to you but kill you and still been able to sleep at night, but this- This fucking act! This will be the fucking thing that keeps me up! I know it. I hope it. I really do. That's why I have to do this."

Maxine tried to move her head from Frankie's grasp, but she couldn't. All she could do was look up as Frankie brought a large, bloody kitchen knife up to his face. It caught the light and shown on him in a rather angelic manner. He was clearly a demon, but then, he looked like an angel who was about to fall from grace.

"I really don't want to," Frankie said.

"Don't," Maxine said.

"I *have* to," Frankie said as he moved the knife from his face.

Maxine could feel Frankie's touch as it moved down her body. It tingled and it burned. There was no pain, but there was something close. She then felt it move between her breasts, down her tummy, and to just above her pussy.

"I love you so much," Frankie said as he looked her in the eyes. She could see tears welling in his eyes.

Maxine tried to get her body to do something. She would have settled for her legs to flail or her arms to fight, but what she really wanted to do was run. That was impossible, however, and so she just lay there, terror over took her mind as Frankie overtook her body.

She then felt something sharp enter her.

---

Frankie had pulled out all the stops for his great unveiling. He had grabbed every drug he could find in the house and displayed it in such a way that would be esthetically pleasing, to literally no one (but himself, of course), on the coffee table in front of the TV in what was once a living room.

Before he plugged the camera into the television to watch what he had shot, he did a little bit of everything. He lit up a joint as he took a swig from a mixture of bourbon and vodka and cut a line of cocaine. It was a rather large line, but he took it with ease. He then moved to a rather poorly prepared line of heroin. It burned his nose as he snorted it up, but he popped some of Maxine's valium to dull the pain a little bit. Before the valium had time to take effect he popped some of his trusty shroom pills and moved to the camera.

It took him awhile to plug the camera into the television, but once he did, it started playing before he was ready. The light from the screen lit up the room. It was bright and Frankie looked away from the screen until he heard himself speak.

"How're you doing, Maxine?" he heard his voice say as he watched himself sit on the bed.

Frankie didn't want to watch the build up, though. He knew he would probably cut all that shit out of the final product he would post online. With that in mind he pushed the fast-forward button.

He watched, in a sped-up fashion, as he sits down next to Maxine and runs the knife down her leg to her toes, cutting her all the while. He watched as he and her have a dialogue and then he brings the knife to his face. Before he pressed play, Frankie (on the recording) runs the knife down Maxine's body.

Once Frankie pushed play he walked back to the couch and lit up a cigarette. He placed it, in his fingers, next to the joint. He took a drag off of both before he coughed.

"I love you so much," the onscreen Frankie says.

As Frankie heard that he put out the joint, deciding to stick with just the cigarette, and looked up to the screen.

He watched as his past self rams the knife into Maxine's cunt.

"Fuck you! Fuck you! Fuck you!" the Frankie on the TV shouts as he rams the knife in and out of Maxine.

Blood begins to pour out instantaneously, yet the Frankie in the recording continues to stab over and over again.

"Fuck you!" Frankie's voice rings out through the speakers. It was loud, almost too loud. Frankie lamented the fact that he might have to sound-edit his voice so it sounded a little softer.

He went to grab the remote control to turn it down, but before he could, it was like the onscreen Frankie was reading his future-self's mind.

"Fuck you... Fuck you..." Frankie (on the TV) says, softer than before. "Fuck you... Fuck you..."

As Frankie watched himself kill the woman he loved the most, a tear began to form in his eye.

"This," Frankie (in the living room) said, as he took a drag from his cigarette. "This is fucking brilliant."

Frankie watched as he moves the knife in and out of Maxine, crying as he does so.

"Francis, stop!" Maxine shouts.

But Frankie doesn't stop. He doesn't know how.

# AUTHOR'S NOTE

I know I'm about to receive a lot of letters regarding this book. I know they're going to be filled with criticism, and I know why. It isn't hard to see. There is a glaring flaw within these pages and I feel it must be addressed here (maybe it will save some paper or, at the very least, time).

It came to my attention, after the book had been drafted and drafted and drafted, that there should be some cause for concern when it came to a certain scene involving Rachel and a horse.

Well, an equestrian friend of mine informed me that horses are not prone to behave that way. I tried to argue that this horse might, given the fact the horse was being touched near its private parts, but I was assured again and again that horses tend to try to escape, rather than attack. When I countered that point with the fact that the horse was in a stall I was then talked down to and told that the horse may knock Rachel out, but as soon as the threat was eliminated, the horse wouldn't continue its onslaught. I then tried to at least posit that the horse might be wild and untamed, like some sort of stallion or bronco. I was then told to shut the fuck up and change the book.

I didn't change the book, though. I couldn't. Call it laziness or call it commitment, but Frankie's story absolutely needed a scene with light-bestiality gone wrong. I did try to think of a remedy, but none came, and so I left the scene in knowing full well I would receive flack out the ass over it.

So I'm trying to fix it here. I'm trying to let you know that I know a horse would never commit murder of any kind. They are peaceful and docile creatures and it was wrong of me to insinuate that they could be capable of malice (even if the malice was brought on by self-defense). I don't want you to think that horses can be mean just because I wrote it; this is a work of fiction, after all.

L. Kurt Eddy

# ACKNOWLEDGMENTS

Now, I know absolutely no one in their right mind would want to be associated with what I have written here, I'm not an idiot. I would be remiss, however, if I didn't at least give credence (or, perhaps blame) to those who helped me get here.

I need to thank my father, first and foremost. Without you I wouldn't be as twisted and fucked up as I am.

I also need to, in nearly the same breath, thank my mother. She kept me alive, for better or worse, and is always a sane voice in my rather burning brain.

My girlfriend also needs to be thanked. Maybe thanked with more reverence than the others. She refuses to be named in the book (for obvious reasons), but I want her to know I'm thanking her. She's cleaned my vomit off of toilet bowls and my shit out of my underwear. She is clearly the woman I have always been searching for and I love her so much.

I suppose, in that same vein, I need to thank the girlfriend I was with when I wrote this piece-of-shit. She read it and cried at the end, because it was horrifying. Even with that thought in her mind, she told me to do something with it. She had a good head on her shoulders. She left me after all.

I would also like to thank my sister. She won't read this, because I won't let her, but she's an amazing woman and I love her to death.

My good friend, James (not the basis of the James in the story), I've got to thank you too, man. You are the Miles to my Frankie. Hopefully, I won't ever put you in the same situation.

Now that my loved ones are out of the way, let's get into the crew I hung out with from my porno days:

Ashe, you were worth it. I mean, at least to a "motherfucker" like me.

Ashton, the pillow-talk interviews you let me put upon you were a big help in the making of this book. More than my "career" in the industry could have ever garnered me.

Blair, you surely can see some of you in here. At least I hope you can. You're worthy of it. I mean that in the nicest way.

Brooke, you too. Just put your name there in Blair's "thank you", you've done it before.

Grace, I mean c'mon, there's a little bit of Maxine in you.

Ida, you're still the best kisser. Thanks for being the first person to hire me.

Howie, thanks, man, for fucking paying me to be apart of your company. I learned a lot there. Sorry I fucked your wife.

Marina, doing butt-stuff with you knocked several things off my bucket list.

Roxy, dear god, without you I would be nothing. You let my creativity fly. The shit I wrote for you is still probably my best work.

So yeah, that is that. I suppose I need to thank the crazy Nicolas Ryan Moore for publishing this and Pedro for pushing for it. Donny needs a shout out. For what? I don't know. (Get it?) Also, Leah, I know you're a prude, but you still were willing to work with me on this. I really should have just thanked Idea Machine Output as a whole, but oh well.

Oh yeah, I want to thank whoever is reading this, too. It really means a lot. You're a special person and the thanks I have for you is something I have never felt before. Feel awesome.

# ABOUT THE AUTHOR

L. Kurt Eddy is a writer based out of Portland, Oregon. He is, for all intents and purposes, homeless. There's not merit to you knowing this, but he wants you to know it. So, there you go.

<u>Frankie's Unlawful Carnal Knowledge</u> is his first published novel, but he has more coming (so stay tuned).

He is open to questions and concerns about this novel (he is almost positive you have missed its meaning) and so you can email him at lkurteddy@gmail.com. Please drop him a line for all civil discourses/death threats.

This has been a publication from:

**Idea Machine Output**.

Idea Machine Output is a collective of writers and artists based in The Pacific Northwest. They produce books, films, and other materials.

For more information feel free to visit their website: IdeaMachineOutput.com or email them at info@ideamachineoutput.com.